USA TODAY BESTSELLING AUTHOR
DALE MAYER

Revenge in the Roses

Lovely Lethal Gardens 18

REVENGE IN THE ROSES: LOVELY LETHAL GARDENS, BOOK 18
Beverly Dale Mayer
Valley Publishing Ltd.

ISBN-13: 978-1-773366-48-7
Print Edition

Books in This Series

About This Book

A new cozy mystery series from *USA Today* best-selling author Dale Mayer. Follow gardener and amateur sleuth Doreen Montgomery—and her amusing and mostly lovable cat, dog, and parrot—as they catch murderers and solve crimes in lovely Kelowna, British Columbia.

Riches to rags. … Bullets start flying. … Rage is rising, … especially for some!

When the journey to Rosemoor for a celebratory evening turns deadly, Doreen's life is flipped on her head. She can only watch in horror as Mack is shot right in front of her. Horrified, she vows to solve this case and fast, before the shooter realizes he failed and comes back for a second attempt.

Corporal Mack Moreau has been shot before, but this time it's way worse because Doreen watched it all happen. Now she's planning to catch the shooter before Mack even starts to heal. That's not a good idea. She's yet to consider that maybe the shooter wasn't after Mack but really wanted to shoot her. After all, the cases she's been involved in have created a whole new level of acquaintances in her life. How many of them are gunning for her?

But Doreen is not deterred, and, with her trusty team at her side, she's determined to keep Mack safe by finding his shooter before he tries again.

Sign up to be notified of all Dale's releases here!
https://geni.us/DaleNews

Chapter 1

Late August, Tuesday Evening

A FEW DAYS later Doreen Montgomery walked down to Nan's with Mack Moreau and the animals bouncing at her side. They loved to go for a walk at the best of times and adored going to Nan's anytime, but to have Doreen and Mack together on this walk heading to their favorite place? Needless to say the animals were delirious with joy. Even Thaddeus struggled to figure out whose shoulder he should ride on and kept switching from Doreen to Mack and back.

"This is becoming a bit of a habit," Doreen noted.

"Is two times a habit?" Mack asked in a teasing voice. "I don't come down here anywhere close to the times that you visit."

"Maybe." She shrugged, too happy to care.

"I have to be there now because Nan is hosting a celebration for you."

Doreen chuckled. "I told her not to bother."

"Yep, but you also know how much she loves doing this kind of stuff."

"Yeah, that's true," she murmured. "She really does have fun, doesn't she?"

"And so she should. It's important to her."

Doreen nodded. "And anything that's important to Nan is important to me."

"Although I'm not too sure that I want Bernard there," Mack noted in an odd tone.

"You're fine to have Bernard there," she replied immediately, "because he doesn't matter to me, not in that way."

"At least my brother has got your ex working on some paperwork. Now to get this divorce of yours settled."

"I know. Isn't that huge?" She clapped her hands. "Also I have a message from Scott at the auction house, but I couldn't reach him directly. Something about the antiques. He said it was good news though." She beamed up at him. "Sounds like we get to eat for another day."

"Yay," Mack said, with a grin. "You got the ten thousand dollar reward from Bernard. With any luck, Nick is making progress on your divorce. Plus now money from the antiques auction might be coming in too. You'll be rolling in money before you know it."

"Even though I'm sharing that reward with Esther, I'm feeling pretty cheeky about money right now," she admitted. "I know five thousand isn't much. But, as Candy said, until you have to sell your clothing to buy food to eat, you don't know what poor is."

"But I liked your response," he replied. "It shows your priorities are right."

"I hope so," she murmured. "How will Candy turn out in all this?"

"Better than I think she expects. I mean, she had physical possession of the real diamond for ten years, yet she didn't know it wasn't the fake ring. Although she technically didn't do anything illegal, she was still part of the original plan to steal one expensive diamond ring," he added, "so that will be the only issue. I've left it with the DA to sort out, but I suspect she will get off with a small sentence or probation, if anything at all. She was there, helping to solve it at the end. At least that's how she put it. Something about the way *you* suggested that she say it."

Doreen shrugged. "Candy didn't complain when I called for the police to give us a hand," Doreen noted, still beaming. "So, as far as I'm concerned, Candy helped solve it at the end, and she should be let off the hook. Besides, she has been going to therapy for a long time, will continue going, and seems intent on rehabilitating herself."

"I know," Mack admitted. "And anything that she can do to get herself back on track is huge."

"I agree. It's pretty sad when we see the same people committing crimes time and time again."

Mack nodded.

As they came around the corner of the greenway, heading toward Nan's, Doreen looked up at the sky and sighed. "It's a perfect evening."

"And everybody'll be there," he said, chuckling. "What fun."

"I could do without all the attention," she groaned.

They came up to the huge rosebush alongside the pathway, leading from the parking lot to the front door of Rosemoor.

She smiled and said, "Aren't they beautiful?"

"I didn't think they bloomed this time of year."

She nodded. "Roses can bloom for a very long time, if they're well tended to. Kind of like revenge."

He looked at her. "Where did that come from?" he asked.

3

She shrugged, gave him a little smirk. "You know, like, *Revenge in the Roses.*"

He rolled his eyes. "How about you just take a break from all these murder cases?"

"Maybe," she said cheerfully. "I intend to enjoy tonight at least."

"Good."

They walked the last few steps, when a man stepped out from a parked vehicle, and called out to Mack, "Hey, copper."

Mack turned toward him and frowned. "Can I help you?"

"Absolutely you can. You can die." And, with that, he shot Mack. He fired a second shot at Doreen, but she had already dropped beside Mack, who'd fallen into the rosebush.

He called out, "Revenge is best served cold." And, with a hard laugh, he added, "And now you're dead too." He bolted away in a vehicle, tearing off as fast as it could go.

All Doreen could do—as she tried to stop the bleeding in Mack's upper chest—was think about her words. *Revenge in the Roses.* Had she helped make this happen?

Chapter 2

DOREEN HUDDLED IN the waiting room of the ER, more shaken and shocked than she'd thought possible. All she saw was Mack's bleeding body in the bushes. She kept getting up and pacing, before sitting back down again. Several of Mack's coworkers, and even the captain, had already approached her and had asked her question after question after question. She could tell them only so much. And most of that was pretty nonexistent. She knew Darren had gone to Rosemoor to talk to multiple people at the seniors' living center, but she couldn't imagine that anybody had anything to say. There wasn't much to tell.

As Doreen had gone over it time and time again in her own mind, she wasn't sure that she could have done anything differently, but, at the same time, guilt ate at her. She hadn't expected something like that.

And the gunman's words also concerned her. Instinctively she worried that the shooting was connected to one of her nightmarish cases, but she had her doubts. She told the captain that she was pretty sure this shooting had something to do with Mack's cases. The captain had a team working on it right now, but still the captain wanted to make sure that she was okay.

He asked her again, "Wouldn't you be better off going home and resting there?"

"No," she replied. "I can't leave him here."

He looked at her, smiled, and patted her hands. "I'm really glad you care, but Mack won't be very happy if you wear yourself down any more than you already have with all these other cases. You've been here for hours." He added, "Plus it's been pretty chaotic in your world lately. You should rest as much as you can. They're taking Mack in for surgery now, but the bullet didn't cause any major damage, so he'll be fine."

She took yet another shaky breath, looked at the captain, then smiled slightly. "I know that should calm me down, and I'm grateful for that. Plus he'd be livid if I felt guilty, but ..."

"And why would you feel guilty?" the captain asked curiously. "Did you know this would happen?"

"No, of course not. But I feel like I should have done something more," she's cried out softly. "Or at least seen something. All I can tell you is the color of the vehicle and what the man looked like, but that's not even clear. He had on a hat and sunglasses, and he had a small handgun. I didn't even see it clearly enough to offer anything useful. We were just going down for that celebration and then ..." She stopped and shook her head. "I don't even want to think about that."

"One of my men is still down there, talking to all the residents."

She nodded. "I know Darren went down there. And I really hope that somebody at Rosemoor saw something, but chances are they don't know what they might have seen." He looked at her curiously. She shrugged. "You know what it's like when a crime happens. Nobody ever sees anything, until you point out something completely unrelated, and they're like, *Oh, yeah, you mean like the guy I saw at such-and-such time.*" She waved her hand around. "It's as if you have to jog people's memories."

The captain smiled. "You've come a long way doing all this. Became quite a pro in no time at all."

"I don't know that I've come anywhere," she muttered. "It seems none of it's been worthwhile, as Mack got shot tonight."

It was a hugely sad reckoning for the type of work she did. She groaned softly, wishing she had an update on Mack's condition.

As if to answer her wish, the admitting doctor stepped out, looked at her, and asked, "You are still here?" And then his gaze landed on the captain, and the doc's tone became a little more formal. "Mack is still in surgery, but I haven't had any word as yet."

"And it's not serious?" Doreen asked.

"It's serious, in that all surgery is serious," the doctor explained, "but, in his case, it certainly could have been worse. If the bullet had been any lower …"

She nodded. "That's the thing, right? I mean, Mack's a big guy. Plus I don't even know if maybe Mack was already moving in a certain direction, such that the shot completely missed the location that this gunman was aiming for."

"Either way," the doctor replied in all seriousness, "it's a good thing it happened the way it did. Mack will pull through this with no problem." But he looked at her and frowned. "You on the other hand …"

At that, the captain stood and nodded. "I know. I've

been trying to get her to go home, but she's insistent on staying."

The doctor nodded, then froze.

Just then the big double doors at the ER entrance opened up, and it looked like half of Rosemoor came striding in. As soon as Nan, who led the charge, saw Doreen, she cried out and raced to her side. "Are you okay?" Nan asked Doreen.

"I'm fine," Doreen murmured, reaching out and hugging her grandmother. "It's not me who's hurt. It's Mack."

Nan gave a nod. "I heard that too. Darren's been questioning everybody at the home. It's so frustrating to think that we were there, most of us actively involved in getting ready for this celebration," she stated, "and then look what happens. And, of course, none of us saw anything because we were so busy doing our own thing inside."

"Of course." Doreen reached up to scrub away her fatigue. "How do you think I feel? I was right there beside Mack when it happened."

"Oh, I'm sure you feel guilty," Nan murmured. "Yet there's absolutely no reason for you to feel that way. You couldn't have known what would happen."

Doreen gave her a sad look.

"But you'll feel that way anyway. I get it." Nan looked over at the captain. "Captain, you should send her home. I went to the house looking for her, and, of course, she wasn't there. That's why I rounded up the troops to make sure you weren't holding her."

The captain's gaze went from Doreen to Nan and back. "I'm not holding her in any way. I'm also not keeping her at the hospital. Doreen's free to go. In fact, I've tried many times to convince her to go home. However, she won't leave

Mack."

At that, the entire group of seniors behind Nan gave a happy sigh.

"Oh, we do like hearing that." Richie turned to look at Nan and whispered, "I want to double my money on that bet."

Doreen gasped and jumped to her feet.

Nan immediately reached over and patted her grand-daughter's arm. "It's fine." She gave Richie a quelling look, and he flushed, realizing that he'd said something completely inappropriate right in front of the captain. And Doreen.

Doreen glared at Richie, turned back to the captain, and asked, "Will Mack be kept in the hospital?"

The captain pivoted to the doctor, who was still here, an odd look on his face, as he studied the group of ragtag seniors in front of him. "Doc, will Mack be let out anytime soon?"

"We'll certainly keep him overnight and likely for several days," the doc replied. "But it will be up to the surgeon himself as to what we're looking at for as a time frame—not to mention if anything goes wrong during surgery."

At that, Doreen's bottom lip bubbled out.

The doc shook his head. "We're not expecting any problems," he rushed to reassure her.

She didn't know what to say, but just because he wasn't expecting problems didn't mean that they wouldn't happen. She ran a hand over her forehead. Then she looked at Nan. "He could be here for quite a while. Maybe I should go home for a bit." Although she didn't know why. Then the *why* hit her.

"I need to take care of the animals. As soon as Mack was taken away, I tried to get into the ambulance with him, but they wouldn't let me because of the animals," she said in outrage. "Like, I don't get it. Why wouldn't the animals be allowed?"

The captain just stared at her.

Her shoulders sagged. "Okay, fine. I'm not being reasonable."

"And that's a sure sign," replied the captain, "that you need to go home and rest. If Mack's conscious, I'll get him to call you. If he's not conscious, I'm sure you'll find out how he's doing later this evening."

"Meaning, I'm also not family, so I won't be allowed in to see him." She groaned and then looked at the captain. "Did you phone his brother and his mother?"

"I phoned Millicent, and somebody has contacted his brother. I believe he's on his way up here."

"Right, he lives down on the coast."

Hating herself for her errant thoughts about how to avoid Nick, she realized she would have to deal with Nick as well, which made the decision for her at this moment. "Considering the ordeal I've got coming now," she muttered, "I might as well go home and try and get some rest." But she hesitated, looking around at the ER staging area, even though she knew that Mack wasn't here.

At that, the captain got up. "I'll send you home in a cruiser. I promise, if anybody hears anything, we'll let you know."

She looked up at him gratefully. "Thank you." And then she caught Nan trying to poke her head around various curtains to see who all was inside the ER.

Doreen grabbed her grandmother's arm and asked in a low voice, "What are you doing?"

"Checking to see who's having trouble today," she said

in a chatty voice. "You never know who you'll find in a place like this."

Doreen rolled her eyes, as the admitting doctor's gaze widened. Doreen winced and apologized. "I'm sorry. I'll take them out of here."

He nodded slowly. "That's an interesting group of friends you have."

"Not just me." Doreen laughed. "They're also here to support Mack."

"Oh, absolutely we are." Richie nodded. "Although my grandson told me to stay home."

The captain looked at him and sighed. "And, of course, that wasn't something you were willing to do, *huh*?"

"No, of course not, not if Doreen's here," Richie replied. "That's where the action is. And, if poor Mack's been hurt, we all must stand in solidarity behind him."

The captain suddenly caught sight of the large Rosemoor bus outside the main entrance door. "Did you guys commandeer the bus? Who drove?" he asked suspiciously.

At that, they all just gave him an innocent look.

"We all have driver's licenses," Nan murmured.

Doreen groaned. "Okay, if nothing else, that's my cue to get them all home again." She turned to look at the group of seniors. "Whoever drove, without naming names, get your butt back into that vehicle," she stated, with a note of authority. "And let's get everybody safely to Rosemoor."

"You too, my dear." Nan studied her. "You are looking peaked."

"Thanks, Nan." Doreen rubbed her temples. Just what she wanted to hear right now. But, with that, she apologized to the captain. "Maybe give me a hand?"

Together they quickly ushered the entire gang—at least twelve who had shown up—out the front door of the hospital. Doreen made sure to smile gently at each and every one of them because she knew that they had come, acting from the heart.

Well, that and curiosity, but she wouldn't go there right now. It was imperative to get them out of the emergency room lobby, which is where they were clogging up the space.

As soon as they got them all back on the bus, Doreen whispered to Nan, "Please tell me that you're not driving."

"I drove here." Nan gave her a big cackle. "I'll drive home too." And, with that, she hopped into the driver's seat and shooed Doreen off and then closed the door on her.

Doreen looked over at the captain. "If you've got that cruiser here …"

"To heck with that. I've got my car. We'll follow them to make sure they get there, and then I'll drive you home."

"Thanks. I do need to go get the animals."

"Okay, so I'll drive you home first, then check that the bus made it to Rosemoor." He nodded and quickly walked her over to where his vehicle was parked. When she got into the front seat of the cruiser, she smiled. "You know that this will just get the gossip going again."

He laughed. "With that gang who broke out from Rosemoor, the gossip is already flowing."

"They're all very good-hearted, and they're enjoying life, which is something to be thankful for."

He looked at her and then slowly nodded. "You know what? My mother lived in Rosemoor. I don't remember her ever having quite so much fun as this gang is."

"It's Nan. She rallies everybody into having fun, whether they know it or not," Doreen teased, still with a big smile. "And she definitely comes from heart, so it's hard to argue with her."

"No, I agree with you there. Both your grandmother and

you have certainly shaken things up around town."

"I didn't plan on it," she said sadly, "and I certainly didn't plan on Mack getting hurt."

"Mack's a big boy. He'll be a lot more careful next time."

"But there was nothing to be careful about." She pondered the event yet again. "That was the weird thing. I think the gunman was there waiting for us."

"But how would he have known you two would be there?"

She frowned at that, turning to glance out the passenger window, and then shrugged. "I don't know. I don't know who my grandmother might have spoken to, who all she may have encouraged to come. And surely all the Rosemoor residents have family in town, who else might have been invited too. I don't know if the shooter heard about it by word of mouth. And with the gossip about me and Mack, maybe the shooter just decided he would stop in and talk to Nan—or maybe speak to Richie because of Richie's tie to the police via his grandson Darren," she suggested, looking over at the captain contemplatively. "All kinds of options come up when we look at it from that perspective. The gunman called Mack *copper*, but maybe any one of you would have been targeted too."

The captain frowned but gave a slow nod. "I hadn't considered that, but I will now."

She smiled. "You're a good man. I really hope Mack pulls through."

"None of that defeatist stuff." The captain turned to look at her. "We must trust that Mack's not badly hurt and remember that Mack's a big boy. He's ... He's been shot before."

She winced. "That does *not* make me feel any better."

He smiled. "I'm sure it doesn't, but I can tell you that, having been shot before, Mack certainly understands the recovery requirements." He made a turn off the main highway.

"Oh, that'll be rough too." Doreen frowned. "He won't be very happy at all. I can't imagine he'd be an easy patient."

"Maybe not." The captain smiled at her. "Unless, of course, he gets to spend more time with you while he's recuperating."

She frowned. "Of course he will. Who else will look after him?" And then she thought about it. "Unless his mother …"

"I don't know that that's even an option. Millicent isn't in the greatest health either. Mack usually looks after her. And, of course, his brother is on the way, so there is Nick also."

"Right," she muttered. She winced, her hand at her temple, feeling her headache returning. "It is not an easy scenario, no matter which way you look at it," she muttered. "I do hope you find that shooter soon."

"I do too. And the sooner we can talk to Mack about it, the better."

She nodded, then she looked over at him. "You'll set up security at the hospital, won't you?"

The captain glanced at her as he made another turn. "And why do you think we need that?"

"Because this guy was gunning for Mack. Once he finds out Mack's not dead …"

The captain nodded slowly. "It's certainly something to consider."

"Oh dear," she replied, straightened up in the seat. "If

you aren't going to set up security, then I'm going back to the hospital."

"Why?"

"Because that guy's coming back," she declared.

"But you don't know that."

She frowned at him. "I might not know that," she argued, "but *I know it*, if you get my meaning."

He sighed. "Yes, I do get your meaning. I'll see who's available, and we'll get somebody down there to keep an eye on Mack."

She smiled at him. "See? I knew you were a good man."

He laughed. "I've worked with Mack for a long time. We won't let anything happen to him."

Immediately she started to tear up. "You know what? I would have said that too, but that didn't work out so well for me earlier tonight."

There wasn't anything the captain could say to that. Thankfully he pulled into the cul-de-sac just then and soon into the driveway to her house. She smiled her thanks. "I'll grab the animals, and then I'll head down to Rosemoor."

"Good idea." He hesitated. "Do you want me to drive you down? I'm going there anyway."

She immediately shook her head. "No, I'm better off to get in a bit of a walk. It will help calm me down. You have my phone number, right?"

"You gave it to me at the hospital," he reminded her gently.

She sighed. "See? That's another reason I need to get out and clear my head."

"But remember. He's doing okay."

"Got it." She gave a mental shrug. "Thanks for the ride." And she walked up to her front door.

Chapter 3

DOREEN STEPPED ONTO the small porch to open her door, when Richard stepped out onto his and snapped, "Now what?" She turned toward him, and he motioned at the car leaving.

"Mack got shot," she said numbly, the hours of stress and uncertainty hitting her.

Not waiting for a reaction from him, yet hearing his shock as he gasped, she stepped inside to greet her animals. She spent a few minutes sitting down on the floor at the front of the living room, just cuddling them. It had been a huge shock to them, after seeing Mack had been hurt. She'd had to drag them back home and pretty well leave them locked up all this time, while she ran to the hospital. Speaking of which, she was not even sure how she made it to the hospital. She frowned at that and realized that she'd left her car there. She groaned.

"Good Lord," she whispered. "I accepted a ride home, but now my vehicle's stuck at the hospital."

She shook her head, knowing that that wasn't even the issue for the moment. The current issue was getting to Rosemoor to meet up with the captain and to talk to that group of seniors Nan had marshaled together. The chaos would persist if Doreen didn't show up. She loved her grandmother dearly, and Doreen knew that Nan was quite fond of Mack, so this unruly community interest would be ongoing, until this case was solved.

The captain might want her out of the way, but she wouldn't let that deter her, not when she had to make sure this case was solved, if only to keep Mack safe.

She almost smiled at that, as she wandered through to the kitchen and fed the animals. She gave them ten minutes to sit and eat. She looked longingly at her coffeepot, but going to Rosemoor meant tea at Nan's. So Doreen was better off not tanking up too much more. Not to mention the fact that the coffee she'd had at the hospital was terrible, and her stomach was not impressed. After giving the animals a few more minutes, she picked up Mugs's leash, and he came running. Goliath looked at her inquisitively, and she nodded.

"Yep, Goliath, let's go. We're all going back to Nan's."

At that name, even Goliath perked up and came running too.

Thaddeus called out, "Thaddeus is here. Thaddeus is here."

She put an arm out, and he hopped on and quickly walked up to her shoulder, his claws a little more grippy than normal. She gently nudged him into the crook of her neck and whispered, "I need all you guys to be good, and I need all your support, so that we can figure out what happened to Mack, okay?"

As she walked to the river and headed down the path to Rosemoor, she was thankful for the man-made light around her, so she could make her way there, even in the dark. The water trickled gently at her side. Mission Creek was more of a creek at this time of year, but could become a raging river at any time. If she wasn't so tired, she'd contemplate why such a body of water could be so misnamed, but she didn't have the energy.

A deep fatigue hit her but so did the need to jump on this case. The shooting scenario kept repeating in her head but before Doreen could begin to actively investigate, she had to get to her grandmother…calm down. Surely someone at Rosemoor saw something. But then Doreen would also love to find out what Darren had learned. Not that he'd tell her. She just needed to know who at Rosemoor might have seen something so Doreen could talk to them herself.

And that was always part of the trick at that place. Who knew what? And who just *thought* they knew something? And who wanted to know something, so they added in a little tidbit here and there to make it sound like they knew more. Doreen considered how excited all the seniors would be, particularly hearing that Mack would be okay. She had to appreciate everybody's concern for him, yet wished they were just a little less obvious. But then that was Nan's way. She could almost hear Mack's voice in her head. *Nan? What about you?*

She smiled at that and whispered, "You just get better, big guy."

And, with the animals cheerfully bouncing around beside her—delighted to have her with them again and to all be outside—Doreen walked at a slower pace to Nan's. Doreen didn't know how long it would take for the truth to set in, but she felt a tension coiling up inside, a tension that said something was rotten in her world and that Mack had paid the price.

Of course that could be Doreen's guilt talking, since she didn't know for sure that this had anything to do with her. As she remembered the gunman's words, it sounded like it was much more directed at Mack himself. At first. Was the gunman talking about getting revenge with her too? Maybe he'd been shooting at her as well. She distinctly remembered two shots.

Her footsteps faltered, as she seriously considered that. What she really wanted to do was get a replay of what had happened, an instant replay that she could look at over and over again, looking for details to solve this. It was hard to remember what this gunman looked like. It was like a nondescript height, a nondescript gray car. Thousands of them were on the road. And it had four doors and a hood and squarish-looking front. She wasn't even sure if any identifying emblem had been on the front of the hood. What it left her with was a nondescript car, a nondescript man, a nondescript everything. So not helpful.

By the time she'd turned at Nan's place, she stepped onto Nan's little patio and noted no sign of her grandmother. Had they all congregated at somebody else's place? She walked through Nan's small apartment with the animals in tow and headed out into the hallway. Again complete silence. Everywhere was quiet. Doreen frowned, as she and her furry crew wandered down toward one of the big common areas. As she got closer, she heard a din ahead of her.

Under her breath she muttered to the animals, "Looks like we found them."

She stepped into the room, hearing her Nan crying out, "We must do something to help. We don't know who is doing this, but we can't have anybody shooting people on our property or even in this case coming to visit us," she stated. "That means none of our friends and family are safe."

A responding rallying cry came from everyone in the room.

Doreen groaned. She saw the captain standing at the front of the crowd, as if he were trying to conduct a meeting but had lost control. His gaze searched the room in consternation and then landed on her. At that, his face lit up.

"And speaking of which," he yelled over the uproar, "Doreen's here."

At that, everybody turned, looking around, and saw her. Almost immediately loud clapping filled the air.

Chapter 4

WHEN SOME OF the noise died down, the sea of faces in front of Doreen parted and gave her and all the animals a path to walk to land beside the captain.

Nan took one look at Doreen and threw her arms around her granddaughter. "Here she is. She'll save the day."

Doreen hugged her grandmother back, then stepped over to the captain and whispered, "What's going on?"

He gave her a wry look. "Did I look a little too relieved to see you?"

"Yeah, you did." She shot him a suspicious look. "So I repeat. What's going on?"

"Your grandmother is trying to rally the troops to solve Mack's murder."

"And I'm sure you've given her the official line?"

"I have." Yet he looked haunted.

"And I presume they're ignoring you, as usual."

He nodded at that. "I don't understand. Almost all the citizens in this town are completely law-abiding, So, if I say stop, they stop."

The corner of her mouth kicked up. "But every one of these people is old enough to know what you looked like when you were running around in the buff and sucking on a binky. That does undermine your authority a little bit."

His lips twitched and then twitched again, until he burst into loud guffaws. By the time he finally calmed down, he wrapped an arm around her shoulders, gave her a hug. "No wonder Mack likes you so much," he said, with a grin. "I had not considered my reputation in that light."

"No, but, once you hang around with these people long enough, you realize they respect very few things, and all of it has to do with what you've done in life. And their memories go *waaay* back."

Still chuckling, he nodded. "So then maybe you tell them."

"Meaning, they don't see me still in diapers? You're wrong. They do." She sighed. "But, at the same time, they've also seen that I've done a few things to benefit them all, so that has held me in good stead. Plus Nan would not have them treat me otherwise."

"You're not kidding. They have more respect for you and Nan than they have for me."

She smiled. "That's because you still must be the bad guy sometimes. That's not part of my job description."

His lips twitched again. He nodded. "It's up to you to get them all calmed down and to put them in their rightful place."

"That's the problem. They don't go into the proper place," she noted, with a sigh.

Overhearing that, Nan chuckled, turned to the crowd, and called out, "Let Doreen speak."

Almost immediately the slamming of canes on the floor and the stamping of feet erupted, even if at an odd rhythm, as they moved and shuffled slowly to face Doreen. Then the chant rose. "Doreen, Doreen, Doreen."

She looked around her, shook her head. "All right, guys, before you all have heart attacks, calm down."

At that came muffled laughter. She looked around at Nan. "Do you have some folding chairs or a room with enough seats so that everyone can sit down?" And then came a collective sigh of relief.

Nan looked at the others and then slapped her hand over her mouth. "Oh, I didn't even think of that. See? That's why Doreen's here," Nan told the crowd.

"Good thing," called out one old guy, "because I'm about to collapse."

Doreen motioned to the adjoining communal sitting area, where plenty of couches and chairs were. "Come on. Let's all go over there, so everybody can sit down. Maybe we can get some pots of tea or something going?" she asked, looking at Nan. "You want to go work your wiles on the kitchen staff?"

Nan chuckled and disappeared, as the crowd slowly relocated, and Doreen shook her head at how slowly most of them made their way into the comfortable seating area. She looked over at the captain. "Are you coming with me?"

"Oh, absolutely." He chuckled. "You already got them doing more than I could."

"Did you try to get them to sit down?"

"No, I was hoping to get them to disperse."

She chuckled. "Nope. You know the rule about raising horses and unruly kids? Or seniors in this case?"

He looked at her and asked, "Do you have either?"

At that, she burst out laughing. "Nope, I sure don't, but the rule always is, make the right thing easy and make the wrong thing difficult."

An odd look took over his face as the captain contemplated that. "You know something? I think that goes for any situation."

"Yep, now stay close, while we figure this out. We must take the wind out of their sails, otherwise they'll be all on a big rampage."

Following the crowd, Doreen spotted Darren. She waved at him. "Darren, did you get an update from the hospital?"

He nodded and joined her and the captain. "Mack's awake and doing well. He's been admitted into a private room in the hospital. You're still not allowed to go visit though, even during regular visiting hours."

She frowned at him, wondering if that was said on purpose.

He shook his head. "No, it's not me. The doctor wants to keep Mack quiet for the next little bit. Maybe later tonight or tomorrow morning you can see him."

She nodded slowly. "That'll be all the quiet Mack gets. After that, I'm breaking him out of there," she announced.

The captain sighed heavily. "I'm sure glad you didn't say that in front of this crowd."

She looked over at him, startled, and then nodded. "Right. Believe me. I'd have an awful lot of *breaker-outers* with me."

Now with everybody seated in a big circle, she stepped into the center and sat down. All the animals immediately arranged themselves around her. "I don't know how much of the scenario you all have heard, so I'll give you what I know, and then anybody here who has information to offer, please speak up."

She quickly gave an accounting of the walk down from

her house with Mack and the animals. Mugs lay at her feet, and his ears lifted when she mentioned his name. Thaddeus did the same, poking his head out of Doreen's hair, and cried out, "Thaddeus is here. Thaddeus is here."

Immediately everybody laughed and clapped. Goliath just gave them all one of those long blasé looks, stretched out flat, and let his tail twitch.

Doreen continued. "We came around the corner of Rosemoor, saw a vehicle parked opposite the front door. A man hopped out when he saw us, lifted his hands, and called out "Copper," then said something about revenge is better cold and shot Mack, who was already in motion. I'm not exactly sure whether Mack was trying to knock me out of the way or was moving toward the shooter, but Mack took the bullet high in his chest, actually more of a shoulder shot, and collapsed into the rosebush."

She took a few minutes to compose herself, as everybody gave sage nods. "I'll keep the questions simple. Did anybody see that vehicle parked out front? Hands up."

Nobody raised their hands. She frowned at that.

"Did anybody see the actual shooting take place? Hands up."

Again everybody shook their head. Nobody put up their hands.

"Did anybody know that there would be any kind of altercation earlier this evening?" she asked the crowd.

At that, one tiny little bird of a woman poked up her hand.

Doreen looked at her, with a sinking heart. "Yes. ... What information do you have?"

"My knees have been acting up. That only happens when bad things are about to happen," she explained. "I just didn't know it would be Mack who would get hurt. If I'd known"—she slowly stood, her head barely cresting above all the other people seated—"I would have said something to him, but I didn't know it would be him."

At that, several other people laughed, and one nodded.

Doreen looked over at the nodding man. "I'm sorry. I'm not sure what your name is," Doreen began. "Have you seen this woman's knees cause trouble before?"

"I don't know that her knees cause trouble, but she has pointed out a few times when her knees have hurt, and bad things have happened."

She stared at him for a moment. "Interesting. Okay. Besides that set of knees, does anybody else have anything to add about this?"

At that, several people put up their hands.

"Thank you for all being so mannerly." She pointed to the one gentleman. "I think your name is Uriah?"

He nodded, seemingly pleased that she knew his name. "I want to know what we'll do about it." He then stood. "It's one thing to get all the initial layout of the crime and then ask for answers, but do you have a plan yet?"

At the word *yet*, she realized just how much they were all counting on her. She looked over at the captain.

"I'll give you the official line," the captain replied, his hands on his hips, as he turned and surveyed them all. "And you won't like part of it." At that, his words were met with jeers all around.

Doreen held up her hand. Instantly there was silence. At her side, the captain swore under his breath. She looked over at him, a question in her eyes.

He just shrugged. "They won't do that for me," he whispered.

She looked back at the rest of them, all looking at her expectantly. "First off, the official line is, the police are investigating."

In response came catcalls and jeers.

She held up her hand again. And once again there was silence. "*Unofficially* ..."

Expectant looks appeared on their faces, and everybody grinned, waiting for her to explain.

"Obviously I'll be looking into what happened. Of a bigger concern, as Nan brought up earlier, we must ensure that you guys all stay safe."

At that, one man laughed. "We're already dead anyway," he quipped. "At least let us have a little fun before we go."

She nodded, knowing full well where he was coming from. "I get that, and I know, for you, a lot of this is just fun stuff, but remember Nan was attacked on a recent case that I had, and we don't want a repeat."

Everybody turned to look at Nan, and they nodded.

"That's a good point," noted one man. "It's one thing to die from old age. It's another thing to have it brought to us earlier by a murderer."

"Exactly," Doreen murmured. "So obviously I will be working within the parameters of the police." She worked hard to make her wording right, without pissing off the captain and everybody here. "So I will stay in touch with Nan, and you will not take bets." She gave her nan a stern look, then turned to everybody in this room. "You will *not* bet on the outcome of Mack's surgery. Do I hear any arguments against that?"

Immediately everybody shook their head.

"Not about the surgery, my dear. That's totally fair," Nan agreed.

Doreen turned to face her grandmother, hearing that cagey tone in her voice. "Or about how soon this case will be closed. We will work it until it's solved, one way or another. We can't have Mack getting hurt again, and we can't have anybody here getting hurt. That person was parked right outside of this building across the driveway, as if he knew that's where the property line ended. It could have been random, but I'm not a big believer in coincidence anymore." She paused.

"And, of course, an awful lot of people know about this place, and they know who lives here and who doesn't." She looked at them seriously, her gaze going from one resident to the next and the next. "If you see anything suspicious, you know you can contact the captain and his team. However, at the same time, we don't want all the police phone lines inundated with people who think that, you know, the plumber is doing something suspicious or something silly like that."

"But how will we know if the plumber is doing something suspicious if we don't report him?" one of the women asked in that curious tone, as if Doreen had made a strange comment.

Doreen turned to hide the instinctive rolling of her eyes. "Fine, just don't inundate the police with phone calls that don't have any substance. And please, I won't insult you by having to describe what that means."

"That's fine," Richie added. "They can always talk to Nan or me to get that point clarified."

"And that's not a bad idea," Doreen stated. "You two could run interference for the police, and, if you find anything credible, then you can contact Darren."

Richie beamed.

Doreen pivoted to Darren, who stared at her in horror. Her lips twitched. "But, Richie, please do not fill Darren's day with useless calls either."

Richie shook his head. "I wouldn't do that."

"No, you might not *think* you're doing that," Doreen murmured gently, "but I wonder if Darren has a different idea."

At that, Richie snorted. "Of course he does. He's young, my dear. He doesn't really understand life yet."

"Right. And, of course, you guys have such great experience, a wealth of it, that, if we're smart, we will put it to good use."

Immediately everybody sat up straighter.

"We just can't have things being manufactured for the sake of attention," Doreen reiterated. She hated to state this so plainly, but it was time for plain talking.

At that came silence. A couple people looked down at their hands, and another couple looked at Doreen in astonishment. Thankfully even more just nodded their heads.

"You know something?" Richie replied. "It takes a very straightforward type of a person to say something like that to us, and I understand why you would say it." He turned and looked at everybody around, glaring at them. "You hear that? Don't do anything just to make it look like you have something to say," he repeated. "You got something to say? You bring it to Nan or me. We'll decide whether it's of any value or not, and then we'll send it to Doreen first." He added, "I know my grandson won't have time."

At that, Doreen watched Darren sigh ever-so-slightly with relief. But Doreen knew that she would take a hit for it. "Fine," she agreed, "and now I'll have a cup of tea, and then

I'm heading down to the hospital."

"Not with those animals you're not," one of the ladies stated. "Can't have them in the hospital."

She nodded. "I know, they wouldn't let me in the ambulance either. Can you believe it?"

And that brought the discussion back to how they should allow the animals in everywhere there were people. Knowing that would distract the crowd for now, Doreen turned to the captain and asked, "Was that okay?"

He nodded. "Better than I had hoped for."

Darren stepped up closer. "Yeah, … except for throwing me under the bus."

"That's okay. Apparently Richie's got your back." She chuckled.

Darren sighed. "It won't make any difference. You know that."

"It will if I can keep them a little bit corralled. And *a little bit* means *a little bit*. We can't do too-too much just because of who they are."

Darren nodded. "And you're right. They do have an awful lot of experience and knowledge among them. But, if they don't know anything, they just don't know anything."

"I was an eyewitness to the entire thing, and unfortunately I don't know much either. But, believe me, if I thought anyone could dredge up a little bit of information to help, I would welcome it." She turned to the captain. "I don't suppose any street cameras are around Rosemoor, are there?"

He shook his head. "Nope, there sure aren't. And too many gray vehicles are in town, without more of a description to identify the gunman's car from all the rest. So searching the main city cameras for the car is not efficient or productive."

"That's what I expected." She rubbed the back of her neck. "And I presume you're going through Mack's old cases."

"Of course we are," Darren replied in exasperation.

"But those cases"—she looked at him carefully—"won't automatically say, *Hey, this guy hates Mack*."

"No. Of course not," the captain said.

"And the other consideration is whether any of these people who may have put Mack on their target list," she added, "could be in cases that I brought him."

At that, Darren and the captain exchanged a look, and she realized they'd already considered that.

"Of course you're considering that already." She nodded. "But the gunman did say, *Revenge was best served cold*."

"And what does that mean to you?" the captain asked curiously.

She looked at him and shrugged. "That it wasn't a recent case and that he's been waiting a while to pick an opportunity to do this. So why now and why Mack? Obviously Mack has done something the gunman didn't like, but why now? Has Mack once again been in the news? Has he been suddenly brought up to somebody's level of awareness? Some person who may have forgotten about this beef with Mack, but now he sees him again, and something's pissed him off enough to do something about it?"

"What do you mean by that?" Darren said.

"Maybe the gunman was in jail," she said bluntly. "Maybe he's out now, and he's made plans all these years to get back at Mack."

"And that's certainly possible too," the captain murmured. "Which is why we're going through all of Mack's cases."

"Of course you are. And I already know that you won't keep me informed on this case." A yawn caught her by surprise. She gave a headshake. "It's been a pretty rough night so far. If we're done here, I'll head to the hospital and see if I can coax them to let me in."

"The doc did say no visitors," Darren repeated.

"Yeah, no visitors but family. And, no, I'm not family, and, no, I wouldn't go and tell them that I was family in order to get in to see Mack. However, I do know a family member, and a family member does work for me."

"What does that mean?" Darren asked her.

"Mack's brother, Nick, a lawyer, is handling my mess of a divorce." She paused, her mouth open, as she stared at the captain.

"What?" the captain asked.

"I don't think he would do this," she began, "but ..."

"Who?" the captain asked.

"My ex."

"Explain," the captain said.

"Robin was my divorce lawyer—the one who died here not too long ago, where I looked to be the suspect. Remember?"

Both the captain and Darren nodded their heads.

"She did my divorce, screwed that up, did all kinds of illegal things, including everything about my divorce proceedings. From what Nick tells me, it negates the signatures on the divorce papers. So it all must be redone. And, of course, now my ex is very unhappy because his easy way out of the marriage to give me nothing isn't looking all so easy now." She shrugged. "Of course I don't care about most of that, but Nick is pretty insistent that I get something out of it."

"Then you should," the captain agreed. "If your ex had any money before you got into the marriage, that's one thing. However, if you helped to make any money during that marriage, then that's an entirely different story."

She nodded. "That's what Mack's brother told me too. And I did help with my husband's business over those fourteen years we were married. Mathew, my ex, didn't have very much when we first married, but he's got megamillions now."

"Then a settlement is to be expected, and your ex is perfectly aware of what a divorce could cost him."

"Right." She frowned. "You might want to look at that in terms of Mack's shooting. It doesn't feel like it's my ex in that Mathew would be hands-off. So, if he could get somebody else to do it for him, that would be Mathew's way."

"But what would be his motivation?" asked the captain.

"In this case just because he's pissed off. And also, with Robin dead, and her estate not going to Mathew, everything moneywise has kind of blown up in his face. I don't know whether he holds Mack responsible for any of this divorce mess or not." She shrugged. "All I can tell you is that, every time I've spoken to him recently, Mathew's one pissed-off person. And maybe he would hire someone to shoot Mack just because he knows that I care about Mack."

"Maybe. It is something that we can't afford to ignore," the captain agreed, pulling out a notepad. "Anything else you can suggest?"

"Yeah, that guy Steve, with all the dead bodies on his property."

He nodded. "That's one of *those* cases. We'll have to go

back through all of them."

"I will too. If I come up with anything, I'll let you know." And, at that, she stood. "I also was wondering if I can get a ride to the hospital."

The captain looked at her.

"I know. You gave me a ride home, but—" She shrugged sheepishly. "It shows how affected I was because my car is still there at the hospital."

"Oh, good Lord," Darren said. "Yeah, I'll take you down now, but you still won't get in to see Mack."

"I understand, but I would at least like my wheels back." And, with that, she walked over to Nan and gave her a hug and a kiss goodbye. "I'm heading to the hospital."

Nan lost the joviality on her face and gave her a hug back. "Take care, sweetie."

Waving goodbye, Darren led Doreen and the animals out to his patrol car. As she got in, she closed her eyes momentarily.

"Mack really is okay," Darren murmured.

"I'm glad to hear that." She gave him a half smile.

"I hadn't realized you two had a thing going."

"I'm not sure we do. It's caught me by surprise too."

At that, he laughed. "Yeah, that kind of stuff usually does."

"I don't know what it does," she murmured. "It's all just a little too confusing at the moment. I just want to know that he's safe."

"We all do," Darren agreed. "Mack's very popular at the station."

She couldn't imagine him not being well loved. He had a lot of heart.

As they drove to the hospital, she asked, "You mind

driving me right to my vehicle? I want to make sure it's still there. It would be terrible if it's been towed away. Plus I can put the animals in there, while I quickly check on Mack."

It was there. She gave a happy sigh. As it came into view, she said, "Am I glad to see my car." She got out, along with the animals, leaned in the passenger side before closing her door, and said, "Thanks very much for the ride."

Darren nodded and drove away.

Chapter 5

DOREEN CHECKED THAT her car was all okay, put the animals inside, promising to come right back, and then immediately walked into the hospital. As she reached the reception area, she explained who she was and who she wanted to see.

The receptionist smiled and noted, "I'm sorry. Visiting hours are over. Plus his chart states 'no visitors.'"

"None? What about family?" Doreen asked curiously.

"Yes for family." Then she gave her a raised eyebrow. "Are you saying you're family?"

Doreen shook her head. "Nope, I'm not."

A laughing man behind her added, "But you know what? If we gave Mack a chance to answer that question, maybe he would say something different."

Hearing Nick's voice, Doreen turned toward him, and he opened his arms. And, just like with Mack, she walked in and accepted a hug. "How is he?" she asked, pulling back so she could see Nick.

"I'm pretty sure he doesn't feel good. I was just in there talking to him." He looked over at the receptionist and asked, "Can I take Doreen up so she can see Mack through the window?"

"That's fine by me, and, if you can get a nurse there to okay it, then Doreen might get a short visit with Mack, but otherwise she cannot go in."

"Got it." Nick led her down the hall. "I was just talking to him. Mack is doing better. He's awake, or he was the last time I saw him. He's pretty angry about the whole thing."

She winced. "Is he angry at me?"

Nick looked at her in surprise. "Why would he be angry at you?"

She stared at him. "Because I didn't protect him."

He shook his head, nonplussed. "It's not your job to protect Mack. I'm pretty sure he is angry that he didn't catch this guy himself."

"Of course he is, but the vehicle took off so fast," she cried out. "It's not as if we had even a moment to consider going after the shooter. I just wish I had a better idea what the getaway vehicle looked like."

"Did you see it?" he asked curiously.

"I was there with Mack when he got shot," she replied, surprised. "Didn't you know that?"

"No, Mack didn't tell me that." He frowned, as if not liking the idea.

She considered that for a moment. "That's interesting."

"It is, isn't it? But then Mack is well-known for protecting you."

"Maybe even when he shouldn't," she muttered. Nick looked at her again, as they walked up to Mack's hospital room. She shrugged. "I don't know what to say, but Mack is forever bailing me out of trouble."

Nick's lips twitched at that. "You could try not getting into trouble."

"I could"—she gave him eye roll—"if I thought it would save Mack from getting into trouble."

Nick nodded. "I can't imagine how it must have felt watching Mack go down," Nick said, his voice thickening with emotion.

"It was terrible," she murmured. "Absolutely terrible. But he was still conscious and swearing, so I figured that he wasn't too badly hurt. But it's … it's afterward, when you find out he's had to go in for surgery, and you listen to all those people in the waiting room talking about all the things that can go wrong. And the doctors always give you these big warnings about how there's always a risk to surgery. So what are you supposed to do? You trust in the doctor and hope that your trust isn't misplaced."

"Oh, I get it," Nick agreed. "I flew up as soon as I heard, but thankfully I did get a chance to talk to Mack and to see for myself that he'll be okay."

At that, he motioned toward the hospital room door with a small window. "If you look through the window, you'll see him."

She did; there he was. She stared for a long moment, then gave a happy sigh. "He looks the same. He's sleeping, so I won't disturb him."

At that, a voice behind them snapped, "No, you definitely won't."

Doreen turned to see a cop standing there. "Are you standing guard?"

He stared at her for a long moment. "Who are you?"

"I'm Doreen."

A heavy sigh escaped the cop. "Of course you're Doreen. You do know that everybody warned me about how you would try to get in to see Mack, even when you're not

41

allowed," he explained. "And yet now you're being a little too reasonable, so you're making me suspicious."

She frowned. "Can one be too reasonable?" she asked curiously. He just glared at her, and she shrugged. "I'm happy the captain put a guard on Mack. And maybe you could, … when you see Mack awake again, tell him that I was here?"

His face softened. "I can do that, but I won't let you in there."

"Don't worry about it." And, with one last glance at the sleeping Mack, she turned back to Nick. "Are you staying for a few days?"

"I am. I'll be at Mom's house."

"Oh, good. I'm sure this has been absolutely devastating for her too."

"It has, indeed. I asked if she wanted to come down here, but she's really not very mobile right now, so I came first to make sure there was a reason to come."

"And, of course, Mack is healing now, so maybe there isn't any urgency."

"As a mother, she'd be here in a heartbeat," Nick stated firmly. "But I did manage to convince her that it would be better to see Mack in the morning—after he'd had some sleep, and we knew more."

"Knew more?"

"Knew more," Nick repeated.

"Like, answers from the doctor about the surgery?" Doreen asked.

"I've already had that. They removed the bullet, and it's a relatively minor injury, but they'll keep him here overnight and see how he is tomorrow."

"Right, another worry is how will Mack handle being

home alone."

"I thought maybe I would stay with him for a few days." Nick looked at her, with a smile. "Unless I'll be in the way."

She stared at him uncomprehendingly for a moment. "If you mean me, I won't move in to look after him, but I could come back and forth and check on him. However, if you're looking at me to provide the chicken soup for the injured person, well ..." She winced. "Let's just say, Mack would need to tell me how to make that chicken soup."

Nick burst out laughing. "Mack has told me about you guys' cooking lessons."

"Yeah," she muttered. "It would be nice on a day like today if I had learned enough to go home and to make him something special, but I'm not there yet."

"And it's not an issue either," Nick confirmed. "The last thing Mack would want is for you to fuss over him."

She looked at Mack's brother; then her lips twitched. "Really? I suspect that that's only partially true. When you're not feeling great, I think everybody likes a little bit of fussing, even if they say they don't."

"Now that's true," Nick agreed, with a nod. "You're quite right there."

She smiled. "I do have my vehicle out in the parking lot, so I will go home, especially since I've got all the animals with me. I need to try to sleep for a bit. I'll call Mack later."

"You do that. And I'll stop by your house tomorrow morning."

"Good, I would like to hear an update on Mack early in the morning."

"You mean, you won't phone right off the bat?"

She winced. "Yeah, I probably will. Not that it'll do me any good because they still may not give that medical information to me.'

"True enough, so how about I call the hospital instead, and then I'll update you?"

"Good enough." She smiled. "And give your mother a hug for me. I know how worried she must be right now."

He smiled. "If you want to stop by and say hi to her, I don't think that would go amiss either," he said gently.

She pondered it. "Maybe, but it's so late."

And, with that, she headed back out to where she'd left all her animals in her car. She quickly hopped into her vehicle. The animals surged all around her, and she felt tears drop on her cheeks.

"I know, guys. I know. It was Mack this time. It was Mack who's been shot."

And that just hurt her in ways that she hadn't even expected. She almost wanted her soon-to-be ex-husband responsible for this, so that she could pound on Mathew, could yell at him, and could rail at him for having hurt somebody who mattered to her. But then Doreen realized very quickly that chances were it wasn't her ex and that she was just looking for an outlet.

Plus, Mathew seemed like a possible target because she had so many issues still with him. All she wanted to do was have him go away, like so much else in her life. But it wasn't looking good. At least not anytime soon. Once back home, she put on the teakettle and slumped in place. And then, bolstering up her courage, she quickly phoned Mack's mother. As soon as she answered the phone, Doreen told her how sorry she was.

Millicent sighed. "I would have gone down to see him immediately, but he was taken right into surgery. And, so far, he hasn't woken up."

"I just saw Nick at the hospital, and I did peek in the window at Mack. However, honestly, there isn't anything you can do. He's sleeping. I'm not allowed in to see him."

"Isn't that just a shame? Hopefully he won't be there for long."

"No, I hope not. Anyway I just wanted to let you know, if I can do something to help you get through this, just ask me."

Millicent, her voice stronger than expected, said, "Oh, there is, and it's something you're really good at."

"What's that?" Doreen asked curiously.

"You solve this," Millicent snapped. "You make sure that that person is put behind bars, so he can never hurt my Mack again." And, with that, Millicent hung up on Doreen.

Chapter 6

Wednesday Morning

THE NEXT MORNING Doreen woke, groggy-eyed and sore. She had absolutely no reason to be sore, so it made no sense. Even after a hot shower, she was as achy as she was when she first decided to go for it. She sighed and quickly dressed and moved downstairs to put on coffee. She checked her watch and realized it was almost 8:00 a.m. already. The coffee just started to drip when her phone rang. She snatched it up, thinking it would be Nick.

Mack's voice came from the other end of the phone.

"What are you doing talking?" She gasped.

After a moment of silence, he chuckled. "Good morning to you too."

She reached up her free hand, rubbed her temple, and groaned. "Good morning. How are you feeling?"

"I've been better," he murmured, "but I'm okay."

"You certainly sent everybody into a spin."

"Not on purpose. I know my mother has been quite worried too."

"Of course. You are her son. She loves you dearly. At least Nick is here for her."

"I know that he was supposed to phone you this morning and to let you know how I was doing, but I thought I'd call you instead."

"I'm glad you did call. I haven't been awake all that long after a pretty rough night, so I was kind of expecting Nick's call, but this is much better anyway."

"Not to worry. I'm okay. I don't know when I'll get out of here, but the surgery went well. So some time is required to heal fully, but hopefully that won't take too long."

"Yeah, you say that, but they always talk about shoulder injuries being the worst."

"They can be," he said cheerfully, "but I don't think this one's all that bad."

"I'm not so sure at all. By the way," she hesitated, then asked, "do you remember anything?"

"I remember being shot. It all happened so fast, but I have had time to register the details. It was a silver Camry. I didn't recognize the shooter, but he's probably about five-eight, wore jeans and a T-shirt and one of those plaid lumber jackets, open over his shirt, and a baseball cap with sunglasses."

She stopped and stared at the phone. "Good Lord. You remembered all that?"

"Sure. Why not?"

"I didn't," she said in a disgruntled tone.

He chuckled softly. "It is something that I've been doing for a long time."

"I'm glad to hear that. I'm sure your captain will want that description, as I didn't have much to give him."

"I've already spoken to him too," he said, Mack's voice gaining in strength.

"At least you saw something. Honestly I heard the shots

fire and saw you hit the rosebush, but, by the time it registered that he was taking off, he was already gone."

"And, of course, nobody at the seniors' home saw anything, did they?" Mack asked, that note of humor back in his voice.

She smiled, realizing that he really was okay. "I'm sure if you've already talked to the captain, he gave you an earful about yesterday," she muttered, "but you're right, apparently nobody saw anything."

"And that's not inconsistent with what we find on so many of our investigations. Either everybody saw something, and it all contradicts each other, or nobody saw anything of value."

"And that's where the problem comes in. Everybody at Rosemoor was getting ready for that celebration, so they were more or less inside."

"Right," he muttered. "I haven't forgotten. Maybe we can try again, when I get out of here."

"I don't think there'll be any celebration until we solve this." And then she gave a heavy sigh. "Which, if the captain didn't tell you, I've been tasked with the job, not only by everybody at Rosemoor but also by your mother."

"What?"

"Yeah. Everybody's expecting me to solve this." She heard him spluttering in the background. "And I know you're already in the hospital, but don't give yourself a heart attack over this. It's kind of expected—I guess, in a way—but I can't say that I'm really looking forward to trying to get any information because—if this is related to one of your old cases—you know nobody at the station will let me in on their investigation."

"And not only will they *not* let you in on the formal investigation," he said, "they'll do their darndest to keep you out. I mean, I have a little bit of sway with them, and they have a little bit of tolerance with me because I deal with you all the time, and, well, … you're my problem." He laughed. "But, when it comes to you getting involved with the police the way you're talking about, that's a whole different story. They won't have any patience for you. And I don't want you interfering," he demanded, his voice gaining more strength. "I do want a job to go back to."

She immediately winced. "And I want you to stop worrying," she ordered. "You're the one who's in the hospital, not me."

"Yeah, isn't that a change?"

"See? You already feel worse."

"I do not."

"You do."

"I don't," he snapped, his voice booming through the phone at a timbre she wasn't used to.

"If you weren't so upset, you wouldn't be yelling at me," she muttered.

He stopped and then, in a calmer voice, said, "Okay, you get points for that one."

"Right. So you stay calm and stay in the hospital and be good and recuperate, and I'll stay out of your way."

"Meaning, you won't come visit?"

"I'll probably be too busy."

"Doing what?"

And such suspicion filled his voice that she laughed. "You don't trust me, do you?"

"I trust that you'll do whatever you think you need to do," he roared, "but I don't trust that whatever you think you need to do will be the best thing for you."

She blinked several times. "Good Lord, how can you confuse me when you're not even here beside me?"

"All too easily," he muttered. "I'm getting out of the hospital as soon as I can."

"Sure, but it won't be that fast," she argued. "And you need to stay in as long as you can."

"And why is that?"

"Because there's nobody to look after you at home. I mean, unless your brother's staying, and he can run errands for you."

"I can walk. Nothing major is wrong with me. I don't need looking after."

She added, with a bright note of incredulity, "Oh, sure, so it's fine for you to make sure I stay inside on bed rest when I'm not badly hurt, but, when you're the one who's just come out of surgery, you expect everyone else to let you off the hook?" She hoped that Mack would at least understand that he had to look after himself.

He groaned. "You're enjoying this, aren't you?"

She thought about it and then snickered. "Yeah, kind of."

He sighed. "You're still not allowed to go off and to make yourself crazy over all this."

"Yeah, are you kidding? You're the one who's making me crazy. And your brother's supposed to be calling me soon." At that, her phone buzzed, her Caller ID noting his brother, Nick, was calling. "That's him now. I have to talk to him. I'll call you back." And, with that, she hung up on Mack.

When she answered, Nick asked, "Did you talk to Mack?"

"I just hung up on him."

There was silence on the other end, and then he asked slowly, "Is that a good thing?"

"It's not a bad thing. You know how often he does it to me?"

"Ah." Nick stopped, and an awkward silence followed.

"It's fine," she said gently. "Did you have news?"

"Yeah, the news was about Mack though."

"Oh." She sighed, disappointed. "In that case then you don't have news because I just talked to him, and he doesn't seem to know very much."

"Did you expect him to?" he asked curiously. "He was there with you during the shooting."

"Well, he gave me a much better description of the gunman. Not that it's much help. And when I did tell him that I was tasked with the job of solving this, he did get kind of irate."

"Irate?"

"Well, angry," she muttered, "but then that's also your mother's fault."

"What's my mother got to do with this?"

"A lot of things. Yesterday she told me that I was supposed to solve this and fast."

"My mother asked you to?" he asked in shock.

"Yeah, your mother," Doreen confirmed in a dry tone.

Nick sighed. "It's not that I don't believe you. I just didn't want to believe you."

"You have no idea what this place is like. And it's not just your mother. It's everybody down at Rosemoor. They're taking it quite personally that anybody would hurt Mack right outside of their main entrance."

"Right, but then how much of that is just an excuse to get involved?"

She chuckled. "Honestly? They don't need much of an excuse, so it's probably quite true. Besides, I would obviously do something about this anyway. I mean, I was there with Mack, and it occurred to me that maybe this has something to do with one of my cases, and what if that shot was intended for me? Mack had already pushed me out of the way, so there's a very good possibility that he took a bullet for me."

At that came another shocked silence. "I didn't even think of that," Nick said finally.

"No. And that's the thing. Not everybody is thinking right now. Everybody is reacting."

"Including you," he said.

"Absolutely. At least I was. Now my brain's on. It's just not telling me anything." At that, Nick burst out laughing. She grinned. "I was half expecting to see you this morning."

"I can come. I do have paperwork for you."

"Ah," she said, a wealth of disgruntlement in her tone.

Nick burst out laughing. "I'll come by, just so that we can get to the bottom of this documentation too. I wouldn't say no to some coffee," he suggested hopefully. "At least some decent coffee."

"It's already on." And then she stopped. "Unless you don't get here very quickly, in which case I'll drink it all." And, with that, she hung up on Nick too.

Chapter 7

WHEN NICK CAME around the backyard instead of coming through the front door, she looked up, startled. Almost immediately Mugs jumped up and barked, racing toward him, as if he were an intruder. As Mugs got a little bit closer, he got very confused. His tail wagged but then stopped, wagged, and then wagged again.

"It's okay, buddy." She looked over at Nick. "Mugs is confused about Mack's absence."

"Yeah, I get that. However, Mugs has seen me here before."

"I think he's just a little worried. He understands that something's off, that something's wrong. So I can't really blame him too much."

"No, I wouldn't imagine so." Nick reached down and let Mugs smell his hand. "He really does get along well with Mack, doesn't he?"

"Very much so. Mack has become part of the family."

Nick looked up, smiled. "You know what? I think Mack would really like that."

She shrugged self-consciously. "He's become quite a friend. It was pretty shocking to see him shot down like that."

At that, Nick's face turned somber. "I imagine it was a terrible experience for you."

She smiled at him. "You're another nice man. Obviously your mother's done a good job raising you two."

He burst out laughing again. "You do make us feel things. Whether it's good or bad, I don't know, but it feels like we're all over the board when we're around you."

"Yeah, I think I left Mack upset, on the verge of having a heart attack this morning," she said blithely. "I told him that at least he was in the right place for it." Nick stared at her in shock. She shrugged. "He shouldn't have said what he was saying." She grinned. "I was trying to tell him what I was doing, but, you know, he didn't take it very well."

Nick rubbed his temple. "Do you think Mack's hurting?"

"Oh, I'm sure he is." She frowned. "He just had surgery."

At that, Nick took a deep breath. "Did you say something to upset Mack? Like bad enough to have a real heart attack?"

"Oh goodness," she said, her expression changing. "Of course not. I'd never hurt him. He just gets irritating."

"Yeah, funny how that works out." Nick stared at her curiously.

"Meaning that I get irritating too?" She thought about it, then nodded. "You know what? You're probably right."

He just shook his head at that. "Yeah, I'd think so. So do you have any coffee, or am I too slow?"

"I have coffee." She hopped up. "Just sit down, and I'll grab you a cup. You take it black, don't you?"

"I do."

She poured him a coffee and brought it back outside. As she handed it to him, he had a whole pile of papers out in front of him on the deck table. "What's all that?" she asked suspiciously.

"This"—he motioned at the stack—"is a counteroffer from your ex."

"He is talking to you?" She stared at the papers in astonishment.

Nick nodded at that. "I think his new lawyer has wised him up about what'll really happen if and when we end up in court."

"Good Lord. I didn't think any threats would work with him."

"He's really not a nice guy, is he?"

"Nope, sure isn't," she agreed cheerfully, "but apparently you're used to not-nice guys." He looked up at her. She shrugged. "I mean, you didn't walk away when it came to dealing with him."

"Nope, that's not something I would do."

"Well, you know what my last lawyer was like." She sat down with a *thunk* and asked, "And his offer, is it decent?"

"Not as good as it should be. However, the fact that he's negotiating is huge."

"And so what will we talk about?"

"How do you want to counter?"

She looked at him. "You mean, it's not a case of sign or else?"

"No, absolutely not," he replied. "This is the first gambit. A volley, as you might say. He's taken his shot, and now it's up to us to counter against it." His eyebrows shot up.

"I don't even know what would be reasonable," she said in a quiet tone. "You know that I want this brought to an end."

"I do. And I agree with you, but this isn't very close."

She frowned. "In that case, just counter then."

He smiled. "And you trust me?"

She thought about it and then nodded. "I do."

"And why is that?" he asked. "It seemed like you had to think about it."

"I did, but I also realized that, if you do anything to screw me over"—she grinned—"I've got Mack."

At that, he burst out laughing. "You know what? I don't think I've ever had my older brother used as a threat against me."

She smiled. "I don't know about a *threat*, but I know he won't be very happy if you don't do your best."

"That's true enough. And Mathew's offer is definitely not *his* best. He's expecting a counter, and we'll give it to him."

"Good, and, by the way, before all this is done, when would I get any money?"

Nick thought about it for a moment. "I mean, once it's paid over to me or to the court, we could get that done fairly quickly. It's all about trying to get to an agreement first."

She pondered that. "So I could just sign right now, and then I would get paid in a month, … maybe two?" she asked hopefully.

He looked at her in alarm. "This is not a good offer." And then he hesitated. "But you're broke, right?"

And then she remembered something, which made her beam. "I'm not as broke as I was."

He raised an eyebrow.

"That last case, with the yellow diamond ring, I was given ten thousand dollars as a reward."

His jaw dropped. "Seriously?"

She beamed and nodded. "Yes, seriously."

"And will that last you for a while?"

"Well, I owe Esther half. However, if I'm careful, that five thousand will last me for the rest of the year."

"In that case, definitely we'll counter. The question is, do you care?"

"I don't know because the numbers won't mean anything to me. I mean, I don't want to take everything he has, but I just want what's fair."

Nick looked at her for a long moment and then nodded slowly. "You know something? I can get behind that."

"Good, in that case, send in a counter, and we'll see what Mathew does. But don't piss him off because I really don't want to have to deal with much of that."

"He's still pretty scary to you, *huh*?"

"After you've been through what I've been through," she said quietly, "*pretty scary* comes with a certain amount of territory. And it's not good. But, if we can make this all go away nicely, somewhere over the next few months, and I can put an end to dealing with him and this marriage," she explained, "I would be very grateful. And the fact that money comes eventually will make the next few months a whole lot easier on me."

He smiled. "A lot of money is involved. And he's offered a lot of money, it's just not enough."

"And I'll leave that up to you because, if I look at that current amount, I'll probably think it's a horrifically huge amount of money, and I'll want to just sign it."

Nick immediately snatched up papers, so that she couldn't.

She laughed. "See? I won't know what a reasonable

amount is."

"Do you have anything at his house that you want? Like a car? Anything of value like that which you care about?"

She shook her head. "I'm sure he's thrown out all my clothes. I was allowed to take the car I came with and my dog and two suitcases, and that was it."

Nick stared at her, and she watched as a muscle on his jaw ticked.

"You were only allowed to take two suitcases of your own belongings?"

She nodded slowly. "Now that I think about it, that wasn't very reasonable on his part, was it?"

"Ah, no," Nick said. "Not at all. Did you have a vehicle you drove all the time?"

She nodded. "My husband was embarrassed by my old clunker, so I had a Mercedes sports car. And that's only when I did the driving. Otherwise his driver took me where I needed to go."

"And what happened to your Mercedes?"

She looked up at him. "I have no idea, I took my old car when I left, the one that I drive here now."

He nodded slowly, tapped the papers in front of him. "Okay, I'll handle this. But you've given me a lot more insight into who this man is."

"Oh, he's something."

"What about jewelry?"

"I wasn't allowed to keep it. Remember?"

He frowned. "You might have mentioned something like that before. Again, are there any pieces you wanted?"

"No, I don't want any of those memories. They were all from him."

"And your grandmother didn't give you anything over

the years?"

"No, not really. She kept them for me here. She never did like or trust Mathew. So, other than that, there isn't a whole lot from that life that I care to retrieve. Even after all this time away, I've never missed a thing—in terms of things I even remember having back then."

"And, if he could keep wrangling the negotiations," Nick added, "it could be another year."

She groaned. "I'll never get out of this financial bind, will I?"

"Remember Bernard's reward," he reminded her.

She brightened. "You know that is a lot for me."

"Exactly. That's still one thousand a month for five months."

"Or five hundred a month for ten months," Doreen stated.

"Can you live on five hundred dollars a month?" Nick asked in astonishment.

She shrugged. "The house is paid for, so that helps. If I don't buy anything but food and pay my bills, that five hundred covers the basics," she noted. "However, I'm a little bit behind on paying some of those. I'll have to see if that reward check cleared my bank. Then I'll pay those bills." She reached for his notepad. "Could I have a piece of paper?"

He immediately ripped off a page and handed it to her, along with his pen. And she started a list of the things that she had to do. "I should have done this before, but I do have some bills that need to be paid and some grocery shopping to be done."

"Is that all?" he asked.

She looked at him and frowned. "You sound surprised."

"How about credit cards?"

"I don't own any."

He just stared.

"They were my husband's. And, when he decided we were done, he canceled them. So I had no credit cards and, of course, not having any credit in my own name for all those years, I couldn't get any."

"So you don't have any credit now? At all?" he asked in a strangled voice.

She studied him. "I get the feeling you don't really understand just how dire things have been."

"Nope, I sure don't." He looked down at the paperwork, and his gaze hardened. "But you can bet that, after this, your ex will have a much better idea."

"Why is that?"

"Because I'll make sure he understands that now he'll pay for how he mistreated you all this time," he muttered. He retrieved his pen from Doreen and made a few more notations, then picked up his coffee, tossed it back. "I will make this formal and send it off."

"Is he likely to reverse? Like, take away his offer?"

Nick looked over at her and smiled. "Sure there's always that possibility, but remember what I said. He doesn't want to go to court because he'll lose a whole lot more money with a judge involved."

And, with that, she had to be satisfied. "As long as you're sure, because remember. I know what this guy is like."

"I know, and now I'm starting to understand too. Don't worry. Justice does come, even if it takes a little bit of time."

She smiled. "I'd like to think so but honest to goodness? Lots of times it doesn't seem to come at all, and people get away with murder."

"They do, for a while," he acknowledged. "However,

most times, we do manage to make things right."

"Maybe. Like now, I need to make sure that whoever did this to Mack pays."

"And I need to make sure that your ex, who did this to you, also pays."

She looked at him, held out her hand. "Deal."

He laughed. "I shouldn't be doing this," he admitted, as he shook her hand, "because Mack'll get angry if he finds out that I have agreed that you should be working on his case. Yet I know that you'll already do it, no matter what I say."

She gave him a fat grin. "Of course I will. Mack's my friend. How can I do anything less?"

Chapter 8

AFTER NICK LEFT with her signatures that he needed to reject Mathew's paperwork, Doreen got up and made herself breakfast and sat down with her laptop and wrote out the notes on Mack's gunman as she knew them. She added in what Mack had to say about the description of the man. It was fairly nondescript, no matter what anybody said. But the fact was, somebody wanted Mack dead.

Doreen discarded the possibility that everything was geared to her because the gunman had called out, "Copper," plus had been close enough to shoot Mack. Therefore, the gunman had then been close enough to shoot her too. And somebody would have to be a really terrible shot in order to have made that kind of a mistake. She also didn't recognize the shooter. But somebody, somewhere, *did*. At that, she picked up the phone and called her nan.

As soon as Nan answered in a bright, cheerful voice, Doreen asked, "Anybody got anything new down there?"

"Nope. We're all kind of waiting on you for a direction."

"That would be nice. All I have is a vehicle, which is a silver Camry. And a five-eight gunman in somewhat of a disguise."

"Right, that's not enough to go on."

"No, it isn't, and, of course, Mack has given that description to the cops as well."

"Of course. At least you've talked to him though, right? He's okay?"

"Yep, sure have. And he's itching to get home."

At that, Nan laughed. "Of course he is," she said affectionately. "Nobody wants to be in the hospital."

"Nope, maybe he'll remember that the next time I'm in there."

There was silence, and then her grandmother cried out, "Oh, I do hope you don't have to go back."

"Me too." Doreen sighed gently. "What I do need is a break in this case. I need somebody who may have been working yesterday but who wasn't at the meeting, even staff," she noted. "Do you know anybody who wasn't there?"

"Oh, you know what? We were just talking about that, saying that we had to contact Laura to let her know the outcome of the meeting."

"Why is that?"

"She's one of the nice housekeeping ladies here, but she left early that day."

"Okay. Do you have a phone number?"

"Sure, we're quite close to her," Nan said. "So it's one of the reasons we wrote down a note about talking to her, making sure that she knew how the meeting went."

"And you think she's interested in that meeting?" she asked curiously.

"Absolutely. And she thinks Mack is *mucho hombre*."

"Whatever that means," she muttered.

"*Quite the man.*" Nan giggled. "So, you see, my dear. If you don't nab Mack, there will be lots of other women who will."

"Right, fully warned and all that."

"Exactly. So don't, don't let any moss grow under your feet. He's quite an eligible male."

"And how old is this Laura?"

"She has to be, I don't know, maybe sixty?" she said doubtfully. "I don't know. She's pretty young."

Relatively speaking. Hearing that, Doreen frowned and shook her head. "I'm not too sure that I have to worry about her in Mack's case."

"No, but you can't afford to get too cheeky about it either," Nan scolded, "because there'll always be somebody out there ready to take what you have."

"I know, Nan. I do know that. Do you have a phone number for Laura?"

"You'll call her?" she asked excitedly.

"When is she due back at work?"

"She's off for today as well, so you'd have to catch her at home."

"Okay," Doreen muttered. "Do you know what time she got off work yesterday?"

"*Hmm*, about six o'clock, I think. It would have been just before you got there."

"Exactly. So I'll call her." After talking with her grandmother for a few minutes, Doreen hung up and quickly dialed the number her grandmother had given her. When a woman answered, Doreen identified herself.

The other woman cried out, "Oh my. You're Nan's granddaughter."

"I am, indeed. And I understand you were working yesterday."

"Yes, yes, that's right. I work every Tuesday."

"And did you happen to see a man sitting out in front of the building in a silver Camry?"

"Out front?"

"Out front of Rosemoor, when you left to go home from work," Doreen repeated. "There was a vehicle parked across from the rosebush."

"Yes, that's right. A man was sitting there. I didn't know who he was. I even asked him if he needed anything, since I have worked there for such a long time that I know most of the residents. So, if he was looking to find someone in particular, I could help him."

At that, Doreen straightened. "Interesting. What did he say?"

"He was waiting to see somebody, but it was early yet."

"Ah." Doreen thought about it for a long moment. "But was he waiting to go inside?"

"That's what I think, yes. Why?"

"Because I ... I don't know if you heard yet," Doreen hesitated, then added, "but Corporal Mack Moreau was shot outside of Rosemoor last night."

After a series of shocked gasps, then the woman started to cry. "Oh my, I didn't know. I didn't know," she cried out hysterically.

"And why would you? You were off duty, and it happened at Rosemoor," Doreen muttered. "So how would you know?"

"But it's Mack." She continued to sob. "He's such a beautiful man."

Doreen stared at the phone. "You're right. He is. However, he'll be okay. He was shot high in the chest, more like his shoulder, but this man was waiting for him."

At that, Laura went silent for a moment. "But he told

me that he was waiting for somebody inside."

"And that's possible. That's very possible," Doreen said. "I'm just trying to figure out what he looked like."

"I don't know. He had on sunglasses and a baseball cap."

"But it was a man?"

"Yes, it was a man. Other than that, I don't know what to tell you."

"Was the inside of the car messy or clean?"

"It was a normal-looking car."

"So it wasn't full of fast-food wrappers or anything?"

"No, nothing like that. He was talking on his cell phone. I didn't mean to interrupt him, and I waited a little bit, but he seemed to be a little angry about the phone conversation. When he hung up, he still seemed kind of angry, but I decided I should probably be nice and ask him if he needed something," she explained.

"And did you hear any names mentioned?"

"I heard something about *Bowman*."

"Interesting. And did he give you a first name?"

"He was talking to a man, I think, when I was standing there, waiting. I think I heard him call him *Wilson*."

"Interesting. So he said to this Wilson guy, *call Bowman*. Okay. And did you get this guy's name at all?"

"No. But I was standing there, and he had a notepad with a name written at the top. Something about Lenny. I didn't get the rest of it. Now I'm so sorry. I should never have talked to him."

"I'm not so sure about that," Doreen said in surprise, "because you're the first person to give me any information that is helpful."

"Really?" the other woman cried out in delight. "Seriously?"

"Absolutely, Laura. I really thank you for this. Do you think you can remember anything else?"

"I don't know." Her excitement poured through her voice. "It all happened so fast, and I was just trying to be nice."

"And I appreciate that you were being nice because it definitely has helped Mack."

"Oh good. Maybe I should go to the hospital and see him."

"You can." Doreen's eyebrows lifted. "However, only family is allowed in right now."

"Oh," Laura replied, a wealth of disappointment in her voice. "That makes sense."

"But I'm sure he'd like to know that you care."

"Oh, I care. He's such a lovely man." Then she giggled. "He's a lovely, lovely man."

"Yes, I agree." Doreen shook her head. "Now, just be warned that the police may need to call you back and to corroborate this information."

"Oh, yes, yes. That's no problem. I will talk to the police."

"Okay, good. Anyway thanks for that." And Doreen quickly hung up. Rather than calling Mack, as she normally would have, she phoned the captain. However, it wasn't quite so easy to get through to the man.

When she finally did, he asked, "Doreen, how're you doing?"

"I'm doing okay," she said cautiously. "Now I don't want you getting upset, but I may have found a lead for you."

First came silence on the other end. "What kind of a lead?" he asked, all businesslike.

And she told him about Laura.

"Good Lord, how did we miss her?"

"She didn't work last evening, so she wasn't there for the residents' meeting, after the shooting. She finished work on yesterday just about the time of the shooting, so she ended up talking to this gunman. Now the question is …" Doreen hesitated.

"What? What?" the captain snapped impatiently.

"Now that we've tracked her down, what are the chances that this gunman will be upset that she saw him up close?"

"I don't know," he answered, an odd note to his voice. "Let me think about that."

"Anyway I did tell her that you guys would probably need to confirm the information she gave me, so she is quite prepared to talk to the police."

"That's good," he said on a dry note, "considering that's a necessary step."

"I agree," she replied. "I was just talking to Nan and asked if anybody had missed the meeting later last night, and that's how I found out about Laura. So now I'm turning the information over to you."

In an equally formal voice, the captain thanked her and said, "Much appreciated. We'll take it from here."

And she realized that, just like that, she'd been summarily dismissed.

Chapter 9

Wednesday, Early Afternoon

IT WAS EARLY afternoon as Doreen sat here at home, wondering about trying to sneak in the hospital to see Mack. But she could hardly go empty-handed, and she wasn't at all sure that the man would want flowers from her garden. It was potentially something that she could do though. She frowned at that, knowing that what Mack would really like would be something like a cookie. She quickly picked up her phone, texted Nan, and asked, **What do you take to a man who's sick in the hospital?** Instead of texting back, Nan phoned her.

"You're talking about Mack, I presume."

"Yes. I was wondering about trying to sneak in to see him, but I can't really go empty-handed. And, although flowers are a traditional thing, I'm not sure that's what he'd want."

"No, maybe not," Nan said, contemplating the issue. "But it is a traditional answer, so I'm not sure if it'd be wrong."

"Right, but then I had this stupid idea that maybe he'd like a cookie."

At that, Nan cried out, "Oh, that's a great idea. We all know that the way to a man's heart is through his stomach."

"It's not exactly his heart that I'm trying to get to," she muttered. "And I can't make cookies anyway."

"Why not?" Nan asked.

Doreen hesitated and then mumbled, "I've never made any."

"I'm sorry. What was that? Speak up. What did you say?"

And Doreen realized she would have to confess. "I don't know how to bake cookies. I've never done anything like that."

Nan stopped for a moment and then laughed. "I'll be up in five." And, with that, she hung up.

Before Doreen forgot about it, she sat down at her laptop and quickly entered in the names that she had gotten from Laura. Doreen knew that there wouldn't be any kind of worthwhile hits with just a single name to search for. This action was more to save the information before what she knew was coming up. Her grandmother was a whiz in the kitchen. Although Doreen could learn a lot, it also made her realize just how big the gap was between what she knew and what she should know about in the kitchen.

And, sure enough, she hadn't gotten anywhere on her research when she looked up to see Nan hustling her way, from the river up the backyard through the garden. Doreen hopped to her feet, opened the back door with a big smile, and let Mugs race down to greet Nan.

"You didn't have to come right away," Doreen noted, watching Mugs bounce around her grandmother. Even Goliath was lying on the path, waiting for attention. Thaddeus was perched on Doreen's shoulder, but she knew he'd switch over to Nan's shoulder in a heartbeat.

"Sure, I did. Better to strike while the iron's hot and all that."

Doreen winced. "What are we striking the iron for?"

Nan gave her a look. "Mack, of course."

Doreen sighed. "You know that Mack and I are doing okay, right?"

"Yeah, but you know something? Taking your first homemade cookie to a sick man in the hospital is a sign that you care."

And, at that, Doreen hesitated. "Maybe it's too much of a sign."

"There is no such thing," Nan scolded. "Besides, you are very worried about him, and it's honestly time you learned how to make yourself a cookie."

"If you say so."

At that, Nan immediately nodded. "Yeah, I say so," she declared in that tone of voice that meant she wouldn't brook any opposition. "Now, what do you have for ingredients?"

"That's the next problem. I don't have a whole lot here for groceries, and I certainly don't have anything like chocolate chips or other fancy things that would go in a cookie," she muttered.

"Then we'll just make some good old-fashioned sugar cookies." Nan beamed. "And a good sugar cookie is worth everything."

Doreen nodded and smiled. "I do like sugar cookies."

But Nan gave her a repressive look. "The cookies are for Mack."

"All of them?" she cried out in horror.

Nan laughed. "Okay, some are for Mack."

"I'll also have his brother here too, you know?"

"In that case we better get started."

And, right off the bat, Doreen noted that Nan didn't even need a recipe.

Doreen watched as her grandmother hauled out the sugar and the flour from the pantry, checked the fridge for butter, and froze.

"Don't you have any butter?" Nan asked, turning and looking at her in horror.

Doreen walked over to the cupboard and pulled out her butter dish.

Immediately Nan calmed down. "Good thing. If you have shortening, that would be better, but, if you don't, we'll use butter."

"I don't even know what shortening is." Doreen was shocked at the whirlwind she'd unleashed.

"It's a fat. We use it in cookies and pastry, particularly pastry, but, in cookies, it gives a lovely change in flavor and texture."

Doreen couldn't say a whole lot to that, so she stayed quiet and did as her grandmother ordered. Even the animals were smart enough to stay out of the way. In fact, all three lined up at the kitchen door and watched. Doreen swore Mugs was salivating.

When Doreen realized that she was following orders blindly, she winced. "Maybe we could just stop a moment."

Nan turned and looked at her in surprise.

Doreen shrugged. "If I'm trying to learn to make these, maybe I should be, you know, making them. Plus writing this down or filming it or something."

A big smile crossed Nan's face. "You know something? You're quite correct." She stepped back several steps. "You should be doing all this mixing anyway. You don't have a mixer, do you?"

"No, I don't. I know Mack mentioned that too."

"I had one, but, when it stopped working, I got used to hand mixing things." Nan surveyed the kitchen. "Yet I think you should have a mixer."

"Why? Because I can't hand mix?" she asked in a dry tone.

Nan cackled. "Oh, you're definitely strong enough to mix, but, if it takes too much work, you probably won't do it."

Doreen winced. "So now you're saying I'm lazy?"

"Nope, not lazy. *Busy.*" Nan smiled. "And, when busy people come up against something that would take too much time, they just don't do it."

"Maybe." Doreen was a little worried that Nan was right. "I'd also have to learn to use a mixer."

"When you realize how much time and effort it saves you, that's an easy step. I used to have one, like I said, and it broke, and I just didn't get around to fixing it."

"Ah, so a lazy people excuse."

Nan then went off in a peal of laughter. "Oh, goodness. However, a mixer's very helpful for everybody. Now we'll have to keep an eye out for one for you. Of course, if you ever get in any of that money, you'll go buy a brand-new one."

"Even then"—Doreen shrugged—"it's not as if I'll know what to do with that money, so it'll take me a while to figure out what I can spend it on and what I can't."

Nan shot her a look. "I hear you there. Still, you must learn to spend wisely in order to get what you need."

"Sure." Doreen laughed. "But spending for what I need versus spending when I don't even know what I need, that's a different story."

She saw Nan wanted to argue with Doreen but held back, and Doreen appreciated that. Still, as she went through the making-cookies process, she smiled as they were finally putting cookies onto a cookie sheet, which wasn't hard to do. In fact, none of it was difficult. Even without a mixer. It was almost an epiphany moment that should have happened a long time ago.

"What's that you're thinking now?" Nan asked.

"I'm just thinking that this wasn't hard," she muttered. "And I could have been doing this all along."

"Yep, you could have been," Nan said gently, "but let's not forget that you're busy."

"Sure, I'm busy, but I'm not that busy. I mean, if I'd wanted to, I could have done this."

"That's the trick to everything though." Nan looked at her in astonishment. "If you want to, you could have learned to cook right from the beginning. If you wanted to, you could have learned to do all kinds of stuff. But the fact of the matter is, you were still coming out of a mind-set where you didn't have to, where it wasn't part of your experience. So wanting to do something different had to be a choice, and I think something new is just slowly coming into being in your world—where *you* have a choice. Over time, you're figuring out who you are and what you want."

Nan reached over and patted her granddaughter's hand. "Now put on that teakettle, so that we can have a cup of tea when the first of the cookies come out."

Doreen looked at her in astonishment. "They'll come out that fast?"

Nan chuckled. "Absolutely they will. And the best thing about baking cookies is we get to eat them first."

And, with a half-laugh, a half-cackle, Nan walked over to the teakettle and put it on herself, while Doreen finished putting cookies on the cookie sheet. She quickly moved the tray into the oven, as Nan watched over her shoulder.

"And that's it. That's all you have to do."

"And yet there's the cleanup too," Doreen muttered. But, as she looked around, she realized there wasn't a whole lot.

"If you have one side of the sink full of hot soapy water, just put things in there while you cook or bake. It's faster. Learn to clean as you go." Nan pointed out the few dishes she hadn't cleaned up. "There's almost no cleanup. And, if you had a mixer, it'd all go into the one bowl, and, by the time the cookies were ready to go on a cookie sheet, you would still only have the one bowl and the beaters to clean."

"I think I'd like the mixer," she announced.

Nan laughed. "I can see that. We'll work on finding you one. Still, if you learn to do anything the long way, getting the right tool for the job just makes it that much easier." And, with a benevolent smile, she added, "Now the biggest problem at this point is how people walk away and forget about the cookies. Cookies don't take long to bake."

"How long?" Doreen asked immediately, walking back over to the oven and peering through the window.

"Approximately ten minutes since you made them a little on the small side." Nan sent her a look, as if to say it was such a shame.

"Yeah, I wasn't sure how big to make them," she apologized.

"That's okay, but most people, if they see small cookies, will take two."

"Right," she said, with a wry look. "And, of course, in

my world, two cookies just means I'm being greedy."

"And that was just nonsense from that nuisance of an ex of yours." Nan shuddered. "Nothing is greedy about wanting cookies. I hear all these people who say, it'll make you fat, and all those other things that are guaranteed to make you not enjoy your food. However, it's more important to enjoy the food you're eating." Nan pointed her finger at Doreen. "Everything else becomes secondary."

Doreen smiled at Nan. "That's because you didn't have anybody in the background talking down to you all the time."

"Nope, and I'm hoping that you'll get enough self-confidence that the next time somebody tries to do that to you that you'll just get up and walk away."

"I'm getting there, but it is a process."

Nan looked at her, and her face softened. "It's a process, and you're doing just fine."

Doreen frowned, as she turned to her grandmother. "Not really, but I'm getting there. And that's what counts."

At that, Nan got a little teary-eyed, and she walked over, gave Doreen a big hug. "You're doing more than just okay though. Remember that. You're doing wonderfully." Then she sniffed the air. "Cookies."

Doreen walked to the oven again and studied the cookies. "What am I looking for?" she asked.

"You're looking for browning on the edges. You're looking for spreading or rising, depending on the kind of cookie, but you're looking to make sure that it's got some color on top. And then, if you're really not sure after the time frame has gone by, you can always put a toothpick in it. Just be warned that cookies are thin, so sticking a toothpick in won't necessarily be much of a guide."

"So just better to go by the time frame?"

"Yep. There's a reason why they give you a time."

"Right, only we didn't have a recipe." At that, she pulled out the tray and studied them. "I think they're done."

Nan looked at the cookies over Doreen's shoulder and nodded. "I think you're right."

Feeling emboldened by this little bit of success, she brought out the tray and gently moved it onto a wire rack that Nan had found in the cupboard.

"Now just switch them out, and put in the other cookie sheets."

With that done, she turned and asked Nan, "Are they ready to eat, or what do we have to do next?" She studied the products of her labor.

"What do you think?"

"I think they look kind of good, but I don't know. I mean, is that all there is?"

Nan gave her a beautiful smile and nodded. "Exactly. That's all there is. You just made your first cookies."

Doreen grinned at Nan. "In that case, where's that tea?"

The tea made, they took a pot to the outside table, adding a few still warm cookies to a plate that Doreen carried outside. Mugs danced at her side, hopeful but ever watchful, in case a cookie accidentally dropped.

Nan then looked at her granddaughter. "Now the only thing to worry about is that, as soon as you sit down, you'll forget about the other cookies in the oven."

With that reminder, Doreen bolted back inside and checked on the cookies. They were close but not quite right, and then she checked the time. They still had about three minutes to go. "I'll stay here and watch them."

"That's a good idea," Nan called out. "I'll sit here and

eat cookies."

She turned and looked at the doorway in shock. "Really?"

"No, of course not." Nan laughed. "You deserve to have the first cookie."

"No, you do. You're the one who made them."

"All I did was help you make them, so I won't worry about who's responsible for what." Nan smiled. "The joy is in knowing that we did it together."

And that Doreen realized was a truth that she could never argue with. That really was the joy right now, realizing that she and Nan had made the cookies together, something that Doreen could imagine grandchildren having done with their grandmothers since time began. And, in Doreen's case, it was just a very late, very long-time-coming lesson.

After tea and cookies, she looked over at Nan, while munching on the last bit of her cookie. "I'll take a few of these down to Mack." She held out a tiny corner of the cookie for Mugs, who wolfed it down instantly, then sat in a perfect position, staring at her, looking for more. She frowned at him. "I don't think cookies are good for dogs. Besides, if I give them to you, Mugs, I won't have enough to share."

"Good point." Nan looked at the cookies and frowned. "We didn't make all that many, but would you mind if I took a couple down to the home?"

"Of course you can." She looked at her grandmother in astonishment. "Remember. You helped make them."

"I helped, but I certainly didn't make all of them."

"You made enough that you definitely get a share." Doreen walked back inside, came out with a small container, and asked, "Half a dozen or a dozen?"

"A dozen," her grandmother replied instantly.

She grinned at her and handed her the container. "Fill it up."

And Nan very gently put twelve cookies inside and stood. "Now I'll go home and have a nap, dear."

Doreen eyed her suspiciously. "Are you sure you won't go back and give away those cookies?"

"Of course not. They're your first cookies. I might go show them off, but I certainly won't give them away."

Doreen laughed. "It's pretty sad it's my first cookies, given how old I am." Doreen shook her head. "But I know that all your friends down there will consider this a very necessary first step."

Nan beamed. "And you did so well."

Nan reached up her arms, and Doreen gave her a hug, once again struck by just how small her grandmother was. As she watched Nan head toward the river, Doreen called out, "I could drive you. You know that, right?"

"That's all right. I need to walk off the cookies." And she patted her flat, fit tummy. And, with a wave, she disappeared around the corner.

Chapter 10

AS SOON AS Nan was gone, Doreen looked down at the
rest of the cookies; just over three dozen were left. She
packed up another two dozen for Mack and put the rest
safely away. The animals wouldn't be allowed inside the
hospital, and she didn't want to leave them out in the
hospital parking lot either, where they could raise a ruckus.
So she told them goodbye and locked them up in the house.

With the alarm set—for whatever reason it seemed important this time, and it was on her mind—she quickly
moved out to her car, hopped in, and drove to the hospital.
She was looking forward to seeing Mack. At the same time,
she was a little nervous about seeing his reaction to the
cookies. Maybe she should have just brought him flowers
from her garden. That seemed like the normal thing for her
to do.

But, of course, why the heck would she do anything
normal at this point? Sighing, she walked into the hospital,
ignored the front reception desk, and headed up to Mack's
floor. When she got to his room, Darren was outside.

He looked at her and then a frown started.

"Hey." She gave him a bright smile. "How is Mack doing?"

"He's doing okay," Darren replied cautiously. "We're all keeping an eye out on him in case anybody comes back."

She nodded. "And I'm really glad to hear that. Mack's a very important part of my life."

Darren's face softened. "But please don't ask me if you could go in."

She hesitated and then asked, "Am I not allowed to go in yet?"

"Only family."

She groaned. "*Great.* Is his brother around?"

"He's in there with him right now."

She nodded. "Fine. I'll leave you to your rules. I mean, absolutely in no way will I get in trouble for this one," she said, with an eye roll. She handed over the cookies. "But please take these in to Mack and say they're from me." He looked at her, slowly accepted the cookies.

She grinned. "No arsenic is in them either."

He flushed.

"I think if I've been trying to keep him alive, I would not be poisoning his cookies."

He flushed again awkwardly. "You know that we're just doing what's best for him."

"Absolutely you are, and I heartily approve."

He smiled. "Okay then, I'll give these to him."

"And, of course, you'll wait until I leave, right?"

He flushed once more.

"Okay, fine, I'm leaving."

And, with that, she turned and headed back to her car. It was disappointing not to see Mack, but, at the same time, if that's how it had to be, that's how it had to be. He wouldn't be in there forever. She barely made it to her car when her phone rang. She looked down, and it was Mack. "Hey," she answered. "How're you feeling?"

"I'm feeling decent. Why didn't you come in?"

"Ask Darren. You're only allowed to see family. And believe me. I'm not family, as I've been told by the hospital more than a couple times."

There was silence on the other end for a moment. "I'm sorry. It never even occurred to me."

"No, of course not, but whatever. I'm at the car now, so I'm heading home to be with the animals."

"Unless you want to try coming back in again."

"Nope, I won't put Darren in a bad spot. And you've got your brother in there. So, if I go in there, he'll want to talk."

At that, Mack burst out laughing. "He just left. He snagged a cookie though on the way."

"Of course he did." She chuckled. "Did you get one?"

"Yeah. Where'd you get them? I figured you for a flower girl."

"And you figured wrong. I might have brought flowers to somebody else, but it didn't seem like the right thing to bring you."

"So where did you get them? They're really good. They taste almost homemade."

She hesitated and then let the words rush out. "That's because they are."

Silence came on the other end, and then he exploded. "Did you make these?"

"I did. Of course I needed Nan's help. But we made them earlier this afternoon. They're still fresh, maybe even still warm."

"That's what I mean. They taste like homemade cookies." And she heard him munching on the other end of the call. "They're really good."

"I'm glad to hear that." She couldn't stop grinning. "I didn't have much in the way of ingredients, so it was kind of like making something out of whatever we had."

"That's what a lot of cooking is about," he said warmly. "So, even though I didn't get a chance to see you, I'm really happy to have the cookies." There was such joy in his voice that she had a hard time not believing him.

"Good. I don't know how long you'll be in there for, so I didn't know how many to bring you. Hope it's enough."

"You can always bring me more," he muttered, his mouth full.

"No. If you're sick, cookies aren't the best thing for you."

The chewing paused. "I won't listen to that. Cookies are food for the soul. The doctors have got all that lovely food for the body," he said, but his tone of voice obviously thought the hospital food was pretty bad. "I need these to keep my soul happy."

"Yeah, I can't imagine you liking hospital food." She chuckled at the thought.

"No, sure don't. I'll be here for another day, maybe two, and then I'm going home."

"Good for you. Although there won't be any cookies left by the time you get back to my place. That's for sure."

"You'll eat them all?" he cried out in horror.

"We only made like five dozen. You've got two dozen, and I've got a dozen still at home, and I sent Nan home with a dozen." Doreen paused. *I guess that means that Nan and I ate one dozen with our tea—but they were small.*

"And that was the right thing to do. Nan has my thanks.

She'll turn you into a heck of a baker."

"I think she thought that I needed to want to do it first."

"Like all cooking, it's much easier to learn when you're interested."

"And not starving?" she asked doubtfully.

At that, his booming laugh broke out. And then he gasped and had a coughing fit.

"You see?" she scolded. "You should be taking better care of yourself."

He groaned. "I'm doing just fine."

"Sure you are," she snorted. "It really doesn't sound like it." She could almost feel the glare coming through the phone at her. And then she laughed. "You know what? This is … This is kind of nice. You can't yell at me or glare at me."

"Is there any reason to yell at you?" he asked cautiously. "You've left this investigation all alone, right? I heard that you gave the captain some information. But nothing else, right?"

"Yep, sure did share some details," she replied. "I mean, it's kind of too bad that I had to find it in the first place. But, considering that you weren't exactly up and around for me to give my information to, I wasn't sure what to do, so I contacted the captain. That took a bit of effort to even get him on the phone."

"I'm sure it did, but he listened to you?"

"He did, and then told me that you guys had it from there."

At that, Mack chuckled. "Of course. The last thing he wants is you going rogue, especially when I'm not there to rein you in."

She snorted at that. "You are the one who needs looking

after. Now don't eat all those cookies at once." And, with that, and a big smile on her face, she very deliberately hung up and burst out laughing. "Now that felt good." She couldn't stop grinning, as she went to open her car door.

"I'm not sure what that was about," a man behind her called out, "but I sure would like to know."

She turned to see Nick, Mack's brother, standing there, staring at her. She laughed. "I hung up on him."

His eyebrows shot up. "My brother?"

She nodded. "Yeah. Don't worry about it. It's a thing that we do."

"Yeah, you apparently have lots of things that you do," he said, with interest, "including baking him cookies."

"I've never done that before, and I wouldn't have done it if Nan hadn't come up from Rosemoor and helped. But she did, so Mack ended up being the lucky man to get the results."

"I had one too," he said boyishly, "and honestly they were great cookies."

"I hope he didn't eat them all yet. That won't be good for him."

"I don't think so." He turned to look up at the big hospital building. "But, if he's got another half hour to himself, he probably will."

She thought about the size of Mack and his love of food and then nodded slowly. "You know what? I wouldn't be at all surprised."

"Where're you heading to?"

"Home. Why?"

He shook his head. "I was just wondering if you were off sleuthing."

"Yeah, for that to happen, I have to have something to

sleuth on," she muttered. "And I wanted to talk to Mack about those names and forgot." She sighed. "Now I'll have to phone him back."

"Then I guess you shouldn't have hung up on him in the first place, should you?"

She groaned. "Maybe. ... I did speak to somebody who'd talked to the gunman."

Nick stared at her in shock. "That's wonderful." And then he frowned and stared at her suspiciously. "Do the cops know?"

She chuckled. "Yes, I was a good girl and phoned the captain."

At that, his eyebrows shot up again. "You got through to the man?"

"Honestly I don't think he was expecting the call would be what it was, and he might have been thinking it was more of a commiserating phone call or something—to give me reassurances that he was looking after Mack. I don't know, but I did finally get through to him. The man has been over to my place and helped redo my big backyard," she muttered. "But I was just trying to be open and honest about the information I did get."

"And how did he handle it?"

"I guess he was kind of surprised," she noted cautiously. "I think he's more worried that I won't drop it now."

"Will you?"

She looked at him and shrugged. "Of course not. How can I do that when Mack is still in the hospital?"

"And if Mack wasn't still in the hospital?"

She gave him a beaming smile. "Then Mack would be trying to rein me in, wouldn't he?" And, at that, she burst out laughing again. And then she sighed. "You're right. I'll have to phone him again, darn it. That means he'll just hang up on me now."

"Isn't that fair?"

"Nope, I think he's pretty well one up on me right now."

He stared in fascination while she dialed her phone. When Mack answered on the other end, he was munching cookies still.

"What's the matter?" Mack asked suspiciously. "You never call back unless you want something. Unless, because I'm injured, you're trying to be super nice, and you'll apologize." *Silence.* "I guess not then, *huh?*" he said cheerfully.

"I wanted to ask you about the names that I found."

"What names?" he asked, instantly dropping all joviality in his voice.

"Related to the guy who shot you. You told me that you'd talked to the captain."

"Yeah, but he didn't give me any updates."

"Oh, so he doesn't want you involved either?"

"What do you mean? What did you find out?"

She told him about the conversation with Laura. "So, you need to tell me what you know about somebody named Bowman, Wilson, and Lenny. What do those three names conjure up in your head?"

"Bowman, Wilson, and Lenny," Mack repeated, puzzled. "I'm not sure I know any of those names."

"These are the names that Laura either heard the gunman say into his phone or had written down on his pad of paper."

Mack noted, "Hang on. I'll write them down myself."

"Yeah, right. You probably took a knock on the head

too, didn't you?" she said, with a snigger.

"I'm still eating your cookies, so even you can't upset me. Did you see my brother? Did you settle up that whole divorce thing yet?"

"Nope not yet. Besides, he's standing here."

"Oh, so now you're visiting with my brother, huh?"

"Yeah, we'll go solve this mystery together. After all, you can't go anywhere. You're stuck."

"Whoa, whoa, whoa, whoa, no, you're not. The captain's counting on me to keep you out of it."

"How can you do that? You can't keep me out of anything while you're in the hospital. Now, what about those names?"

"Now, what about you staying out of it?" he countered.

She glared into the phone. "You know that I'll find out. So the question really is, do you want me to find out with your help or do you want me to call you back when I've figured it out? I mean, it's not like you'll get out anytime soon."

"Yes, I am," he roared into the phone. "And you have to stay out of trouble."

"Yeah, why? He shot you. Remember that."

"I know. Do you think I want you on another floor in this place?"

"Why would he shoot me?" she asked.

A long silence came on the other end. "Did it never occur to you that you might be able to identify him?"

"Yeah, but his disguise was such that nobody's been able to identify him yet," she argued. "So I hardly think that's an issue. Although Laura got a better look at him, so, depending on how paranoid this guy is, *she's* the one who could be in trouble."

He pondered that a moment. "You could be right."

"I mentioned it to the captain, but, of course, he butted me out of the conversation very quickly. He did say that he'd consider it."

"He does have a department to run," Mack reminded her.

"I know. I know. And you're just one of many detectives and not necessarily the one he's worried about."

He sighed. "Of course he's worried about me, but there's no need to *worry*-worry about me."

"Right, no need to *worry*-worry," she said, with an eye roll to Nick. "Even your brother's eye-rolling at that."

At that, Nick cried out, "Hey, you don't get to put words in my mouth."

She grinned at him. "Why not? Besides, if Mack doesn't know anything about these names, he won't be any help."

"Of course I don't know anything about these names. At the moment at least. I have to think about them."

"Okay, you think about it, and I'll talk to you later." And, with that, she hung up again. And then she crowed at Nick. "Hah, see? I did it twice."

He just shook his head. "You guys are having way too much fun over this."

She glared at him. "You know something? Sometimes you must make your own fun."

He stared at her and then smiled gently. "I think Mack would completely agree with that."

"Probably," she muttered. "Did you send off that paperwork?"

He nodded. "I did, indeed."

"And of course nothing's back yet, right?"

He shook his head. "No, nothing yet.'

"Fine. It's just frustrating waiting to see what Mathew will do. I mean, I even told the cops that I liked him as a suspect in Mack's shooting."

"Why?" Nick asked, staring at her. "What did Mack ever do to Mathew?"

"It's not so much what Mack ever did to him, but I think Mathew figures Mack's the one pushing for this divorce."

Nick stared at her. "And did you tell the captain that?"

She shrugged. "I have mentioned it, but I don't know if I gave the captain any convincing details. I mean, Mack is a friend, and Mathew is already aware of him. Then there's you, Mack's brother. Since you've been handling my divorce, obviously Mathew knows about you *and* Mack."

Nick stared out across the parking lot. "Good point. I think I'll stop by and talk to the captain."

"Yeah, you do that. He'd probably be happy to hear from somebody other than me."

Nick looked at her. "Have you got a bad rep with the captain too?"

"Nope, not a bad rep at all, at least I don't think so. But I do have a tendency to go a little off the beaten path when he wants me to do something, like stay out of his way. It's Mack's job to keep me corralled, and, with Mack in the hospital, they're a little afraid I might get loose."

As Nick walked over to his vehicle nearby, he stopped, turned, and looked at her. "And are you?" When she didn't answer, Nick added, "I will go talk to the captain and see if he thinks that your divorce has anything to do with this."

"And let me know, please." When he just looked at her wordlessly, she argued, "That's only fair. It is my ex. And, for all I know, I'm next."

"I can understand that. I don't know that anybody else will though."

She winced. "So you won't tell me what the captain says? … Got it," she muttered. "Once again all alone and nobody else cares."

"Not true," Nick protested. "And you know that."

She sighed. "I tried."

He grinned. "You did. It didn't work, but you tried."

"Fine, if you won't tell me, I'll find out another way." And, with that, she gave him a wave of her hand. "Talk to you later." And she got into her car and headed home.

Chapter 11

SOON AS DOREEN got home though, she grabbed the animals and raced down to Nan's place. Nan looked up as Doreen and her crew approached Nan's patio.

"Oh, have you made some progress?" she cried out, clapping her hands.

"It's hard to say, but I did want to know if anybody had any clue who would put these three names together." And she explained to Nan what Laura had shared. "I meant to tell you about it while we were together earlier but forgot, as we were baking cookies."

"Right, and we had to keep focused on those cookies." Nan gave her granddaughter a serene smile. "Those suckers can burn faster than you expect."

Doreen smiled. "But they didn't burn, and Mack loves them."

"Oh, good." Nan beamed in delight. "But then, of course, why wouldn't he? They're homemade cookies."

"That's what I said too," Richie agreed, as he walked into Nan's apartment, heading to her patio. And very quickly a few other people joined them.

Doreen stared at Richie. "What? Did you hear Nan holler all the way down the hallway?"

He nodded. "Yep. When we realized it was you, we figured you had something to report."

"What I do have is a couple questions that could be very important," she said, waiting for all of them to gather together, so Doreen could report the whole thing once.

When all eight people stood in front of her, she continued. "I'll leave it with you guys to talk to the rest of the residents, but we have three names, and they're all connected in one way or another to Mack's shooter." And she shared all three names to them.

"I don't know if they're surnames, first names, or some mix of first names and surnames, but it's Bowman, Wilson, and Lenny."

At that, Nan looked at her, blinked, and turned to Richie. He frowned, and they all shared a look with each other, as if waiting for somebody to come up with information that she needed.

Doreen nodded. "And, from the looks on your faces, nobody knows anything about these names?" she asked. "That is too bad. I was really hoping that you would have some idea what at least one of those names meant."

"I'm not saying that we don't yet," Nan replied cautiously. "It might take us a little bit for our brains to go *click*."

"It certainly takes my brain a little bit to go *click*." Doreen smiled at her grandmother. "So talk to the others. For all I know, it could be Lenny Bowman. It could be Wilson Bowman. It could be Bowman Wilson, and each of these names could be three completely different men."

"Not to mention there could be women involved too," Nan pointed out quickly.

"And that's true too. We can't assume anything. But

what I *can* assume is that these people are known associates of the gunman."

At that, they all beamed. "Look at that. She's already found people connected to the shooting."

"Oh, it wasn't hard," Doreen said drily. "It just meant connecting with the right person."

At that, Nan nodded wisely. "And that was Laura."

"Did the cops talk to her?" Richie asked, frowning. "She wasn't at our meeting afterward."

"No," Nan agreed, "and that's why Doreen found Laura 'cause Doreen asked me who might have missed the meeting. And, when I mentioned Laura, Doreen immediately got on the phone and talked to her. And found out Laura had talked to the gunman."

Immediately came a long series of oohs, as if that were a revelation in itself.

As Doreen studied their faces, she realized that, for them, it really was. Nobody had heard that Laura had talked to the shooter before.

"We don't want Laura to get in trouble, and we don't want this gunman to think that Laura might know something that she doesn't, so we need to get on this as fast as possible. However, you can't go around telling people that Laura spoke to the shooter and that Laura gave me these names because it could put her life in danger."

"No, you're right about that. We all like Laura. We won't say a word, right?" Richie turned his head and studied everybody else in the room. They all immediately agreed. "No, we won't give up Laura's name."

But the way they acted, Doreen already knew it wouldn't take long for the news to get out. She sighed. "You need to be careful. We want to keep Laura safe."

"Of course, dear." At that, Nan waved her hands at Doreen in a shooing motion. "You'd better run along now, so that we can go talk to people. It's the only way you'll find any answers. I'll call you as soon as I've had a chance to check in with everybody here." Nan looked over at Richie. "I suggest we split it up, and everybody gets a dozen resident names to speak to, and then we'll meet back here in what? A couple hours?"

Richie immediately nodded. "The sooner, the better." He rubbed his hands together in joy. "This will be fun." And, with that, he took off.

Nan looked at Doreen. "We won't have anything for you for a couple hours. Go home and make yourself some food."

And realizing that her grandmother was serious, Doreen laughed. "Okay. I'll talk to you in a bit."

With that decided, Doreen took the animals and walked back to the river. She didn't know about food yet, but a chance to sit and to just watch the river water would help her get rid of that queasiness starting to settle in her stomach.

A queasiness that something was seriously wrong with this world. She just didn't know what it was yet.

When she did find out, she feared she wouldn't like it one bit.

Chapter 12

AN HOUR LATER, after playing by the river with Mugs, Doreen slowly meandered up the path to her house. She had to admit that going to the river had been one of her best ideas yet. She felt calmer, with a sense of peace inside. It was a good feeling. Back at her house, she put on the teakettle and sat down, waiting for people to get back to her. When the phone rang, she jumped on it. And surprise, surprise. It was Mack. "Hey. Are you okay?"

"Sure, I'm okay. Why wouldn't I be?"

His voice was a little testy. She frowned at that. "You sound cranky."

He sighed. "And why wouldn't I be cranky? You've brought up some names that I can't wrap my head around."

"And maybe they're not names that you've ever heard before," she suggested. "Sometimes that happens too."

"Oh, it does. I wouldn't want to think that was the case here, but it's possible."

"And they're just names at this point. You know that Laura couldn't give me any other information, at least not at that time. Although it's probably worth a call back to see if anything else has jogged her memory," Doreen noted thoughtfully, as she stared out the window.

"What are you doing right now?" he asked.

"I just put on the teakettle. I spent an hour down on the riverbank with the animals, enjoying the peace and quiet. It's been pretty chaotic the last few days."

"Yeah, I'm sorry about that. That's not quite how I thought our evening would go."

"No, I don't think it's how any of us thought that evening would go, but, as long as you're doing okay, that's what counts."

He chuckled. "How are you getting along with my brother?"

"Oh, fine. He went to talk to the captain after talking to me."

"Why?" Mack asked in surprise.

"Just wondered if there was any merit that this gunman is related to my ex."

At that, Mack went silent. "Do you think it's possible?"

"Yes. No. I … I don't know. You know that Mathew is not always a nice person."

"Is he *ever* a nice person?"

She smiled. "Not in my experience, no."

"So then it is possible."

"And that's why Nick went to see the captain, just to make sure that Mathew gets checked out, instead of tossed or dismissed as not probable."

"I'm glad you thought of it."

"Right. It wouldn't make me very happy if he were responsible for hurting you. And obviously he wouldn't have done the shooting himself, but maybe he hired somebody."

"And, as we know, it's not all that hard to hire somebody to do a job like this."

"No. Unfortunately it's a little too easy." In fact, as she'd found out, it was way too easy.

Chapter 13

L ONG AFTER SHE had hung up with Mack, Doreen sat at her kitchen table, eating a sandwich, her mind wondering how she could proceed with nothing to proceed on. She still hadn't heard back from Nan, and that might very well open up an avenue, but that wasn't the same as sitting here and doing something on her own. As she let her gaze wander through her kitchen, it landed on the boxes of Solomon's files in her little office alcove. She frowned as she stared at it.

"I wonder," she muttered.

She quickly finished her sandwich, washed her hands, dragged out her laptop, and found the filing system document that she'd attempted to make on each of Solomon's cases. And, with that, she ran a quick search, looking for the three names. In each case there were several instances, but then Lenny was a fairly common name. As she glanced through each case summary where Lenny had been mentioned, she was surprised to find a fair bit of information on this one Lenny. It didn't mean it had anything to do with Mack getting shot.

As she read through each of the briefs, she got up and took off the lid to the box of folders and pulled out the related file and brought it to the kitchen table. She carefully opened the file on the table, and she read the hard copy in her hands, which had more info than her electronic summary. She went back to her laptop, brought up the open file summary, and searched for the name again. It was on the seventeenth page.

She returned to the file, quickly flipped through it, and, using her finger as a guide, scanned through the page until she found it. Lenny had been involved in property dealings, illegal property developments in town here. As she studied it, she realized this was one of Solomon's cases that she hadn't even twigged as being important. And yet, as she went through it now, something else caught her eye. And there it was—the connection she was looking for. She sat back and pondered.

Mack's name was even here. How is it that she hadn't noticed that? But Solomon had gathered together hundreds of pages of his research in these files—if not thousands of pages. And, if she wasn't scanning or looking at this page herself, she wouldn't have seen Corporal Mack Moreau as being involved in the case against this Lenny. And yet, with Solomon's death, everything had more or less fallen by the wayside. His investigations had more or less died with him— except for these donated to her.

The main property developer Lenny Farleigh had been charged, and he had paid a heavy penalty, yet maybe not jail time. She wasn't exactly sure because the notes were inconclusive, and this Lenny person had disappeared from sight. She noted his mug shot in Solomon's file. As she went back into that file, she once again searched for Mack's name, but it had only been entered once.

Frowning at that, she took a photo with her phone of

that entry on that page and attached it to an email and sent it to Mack. She hadn't even considered that something useful to Mack's shooter case might be in here among Solomon's files, but, of course, why wouldn't there be? Solomon had been a journalist in town for a long time, and he'd followed a lot of newsworthy cases for decades. When her phone rang, she answered it almost absentmindedly.

Nan, her voice full of self-importance, cried out, "We've done as asked." And then she laughed, adding, "O great leader."

Doreen just grinned. "And did you find anything?"

"Yes, Roger had something. He knew a Lenny involved in property development."

"Bingo," she whispered under her breath. "Okay, and what did he have to say?"

"He said the guy was hated in town. He used to build all these high-end homes, but he would use cheap materials. They would get the building inspector through to give his approval, and then, in the middle of the night, they'd pop out half the two-by-fours for other jobs, and they'd take away a lot of the materials that had been installed. They were installed very cheap and quickly, so they could be easily removed to move to another job."

"Wow. That sounds like a really horrid thing to do."

"Now, according to Roger, this Lenny guy was well-known for this. And a big kerfuffle came about it all, some fifteen years ago, but Roger didn't know what ended up happening. He thinks Lenny was charged but admits it could have been somebody else. A lot of people did time on that case, but Roger's not sure about the bosses."

"No, but it does give us something to go on, doesn't it?"

"So did we do good?" Nan asked expectantly.

"Yes, you guys did awesome. Any movement on the other names?"

"No, not yet. Those are proving to be a little bit more difficult."

"Same here. If you hear anything else, let me know."

"Will do." And, with that, Nan rang off.

Doreen hadn't even had a chance to put down her phone when Mack phoned her.

"Where did that come from?" he asked, his voice ominous.

"Hello, Mack. How are you, Mack? Nice to know that you're doing fine and feeling better, Mack." She grinned. "Are there any cookies left?" Just silence came from the other end. She sighed. "You don't always have to get so upset."

"You mean, when you find stuff that nobody else knows anything about? Of course I'm upset. You're playing with fire."

"Again. Yes, I know, and you're not very happy about it."

He groaned. "Where did you get this information?"

"From Solomon's files. Remember all those boxes he sent me? It was in there."

"Oh, I remember. And now that you've sent that snapshot, I remember who that Lenny is."

"Yeah, property developer in town who used to get in trouble, was accused of shoddy building material type stuff, like stealing two-by-fours after the inspector had passed the work, letting the home go up with only half the supports, using the rest of building material for other homes." She nodded. "Yep, I've already been there."

"How did you find all that?" he asked suspiciously. "Is all that in the files?"

"Some of it is, and then I used my secret army to ferret out the rest."

He groaned. "Oh, don't tell me that Nan and the rest of Rosemoor is involved."

"Really, are you surprised?" she asked in astonishment. "You were shot outside their home. They felt partially responsible."

Silence.

"Did the captain not tell you about what went on at the home that evening?" She broke out laughing. "Because, if he didn't, you really, really should ask him to explain it to you."

"What happened?" Mack asked, fascinated.

"An entire group of seniors marched into the hospital for one, to make sure that you were okay and to find me to make sure that I was aware that I was being charged with the job of solving this. And then, when the captain followed them back to Rosemoor, they had mounted up this big protest and were intent on doing something to find your shooter, and the captain had very little, if any, control over them." She chuckled louder at the memory. "But then again, when that group gets going, it's a little hard to control them."

"Oh my," Mack whispered.

"You missed something pretty funny. But, if you want somebody else's take on it, Darren was there too."

"Oh, I'll talk to Darren about that. You can bet he didn't give me any of those details."

She chuckled. "Of course not. His grandfather was also in the middle of it all."

"Of course he was," Mack muttered. "I think there's nothing Richie likes quite so well as getting into the middle of it."

"Seems to me they've all found their second childhood. As of now they're all looking for information on this Lenny guy and the other two people. And, of course, Roger from Rosemoor remembered the whole construction scheme mess and knew about Lenny and that just confirms what I've already read," she said. "However, we don't have any information on the other two names that Laura gave me yet. Yet, given that this is somebody in property development, it's quite likely these are associates."

"And that's possible," Mack agreed.

"When are you being released from the hospital, by the way?"

"Hopefully tomorrow. And that's not fast enough. You guys are off and running a little too quickly to make me happy."

"We're not off and running fast enough, you mean," she corrected. "No way to know if this gunman isn't waiting for you to get out again."

"Maybe, but I don't know why he would be after me in the first place. I might have been on the team investigating him, but I didn't play a big part."

"Maybe not. Maybe somebody is doing another investigation, and they think it would be a safer bet if you weren't around to, you know, go to court against them."

He paused at that. "I don't know of any investigation, but it's not my department."

"Exactly. And that's the problem with the way the law operates. You guys have a lot of departments, a lot of different people investigating different things at the same time, without interdepartmental communication. And, in this case, I think somebody needs to check with the other departments." She paused. "So will you call the captain, or shall I?"

"I will," he said hurriedly.

"Do you think he's scared of me?" she asked in a plaintive voice.

"Nope, I don't think he's scared of you at all, but I'm pretty sure he wouldn't want another scenario like what happened at Rosemoor again."

"You really should talk to him about that. I mean, honestly it was pretty funny."

"Yeah, I wonder if he'll say the same thing though."

"Nope, he sure won't." She smiled. "And that just makes it even funnier. Anyway, you talk to him and get back to me."

And, with that, just as she went to hang up, he cried out, "Whoa, whoa, whoa, hang on a minute."

"What?"

"This." And he hung up on her instead.

Chapter 14

NO SOONER HAD Doreen sat back down again, when she heard Mugs barking, racing back and forth to the kitchen door. She got up, walked over, opened it, and peered out. An old man with a cane walked slowly from the river toward her kitchen door. Frowning, she called Mugs back, but he was already racing down to greet him, almost as if he already knew him. Even Goliath raced out the door, heading down there too. She decided to meet the stranger halfway because every step looked painful.

As she got closer, she smiled at him. "Hello, are you lost?"

He looked up, his gaze twinkling. "Not if you're Doreen."

"Absolutely I'm Doreen. Who are you? And what can I do for you?"

"I'm Roger," he explained.

She blanked for a moment and then realized what this was all about. "Oh my. You didn't have to come all the way up here. I could have come down to Rosemoor and talked to you there."

"Nope, that's all right. The doctor tells me that, if I

don't keep walking, I'll die, so I walk. It looks painful, but it's really not."

She wasn't sure she believed him at all because, yes, it did indeed look painful. And it didn't look like anything she would say would stop him either. "Come on in and have a cup of tea then."

He looked up and nodded gratefully. "Although, if you have coffee, I'd rather have coffee."

"Oh, I can put on coffee, and why don't we, since it's a nice day, just sit out here."

He sat down in one of the chairs at the deck table and noted, "You have made such a lovely difference to your grandmother's house." He looked around, with a beaming smile. "I've spent many an afternoon here, before we both ended up at Rosemoor."

"Oh, you've known her for a while, have you?"

He raised twinkling eyes to her, and she knew immediately what kind of relationship they'd had.

She quickly made her excuse to disappear. "I'll go put on some coffee." And she ran inside. "Nan, you old devil you." With coffee dripping, Doreen carried out mugs and cream and sugar and sat down with Roger. "The coffee will be just a minute."

"That's fine. The one thing that you learn to do when you're old is wait. You wait for doctors. You wait for doctor's appointments. You wait for phone calls. You wait for people to have time for you." He waved his hand. "We spend so much time waiting, we might as well be dead because, before anybody gets around to us"—he paused—"in fact, we usually are." Then he went off on a laugh.

Goliath hopped up onto his lap, turned a couple of circles, and settled onto the old man's bony lap.

Doreen smiled at Goliath's total acceptance of this stranger. Yet she heard the truth behind Roger's words, and it made her sad. "I'm sorry. Sounds like you've got a lot of personal experience in patience." She pointed at Goliath. "If you don't want him there, just push him off."

"Ah, he's fine. I like all animals. As for patience ..." He nodded. "Yep, I got four kids, twelve grandkids, and three great-grands. Haven't seen any of them in many a year."

"I never quite understood how that happens, and yet I had the same problem getting to see my own grandmother before, so I certainly haven't been any angel."

"No, but now that you're here, you do spend a lot of time with her."

"I do. It's one of my greatest joys. But I also know that it wasn't always that way. And it's no excuse, but I do find great comfort in spending time with her now."

"And that's the way it should be. And I have hopes that some of my family will move closer at some time, but it is the way of the world. Everybody has to get up and go. They've got to do their own thing, and they've got to do it in their own time frame, and it doesn't really matter what you think."

"I think it matters what we think. We just have to open our hearts and then let others be themselves."

"Exactly." He smiled. "Nan raised you right, didn't she?"

Doreen chuckled. "The part that she had a hand in, yep, she sure did." Doreen hopped up. "Sounds like the coffee's done." And she raced inside, brought out the coffeepot, and filled their cups, nudging the sugar and the cream toward him.

He looked at the sugar appreciatively. "Thanks. There's this huge trend toward black coffee. I like my coffee just fine, but I really do like a little sweetener in it."

"Help yourself. No dietitian is here to regulate what you eat or drink." And she grinned at him. "Just watch out for Goliath. He does love his cream."

He burst out laughing at that and nodded. "See? That shows me that you do understand what our life is like."

"Yeah, rounds of doctors, dietitians, health-care workers, housekeeping, the whole works. And I know sometimes Nan's fine with it, and sometimes she quickly has enough of it."

"Yep, that's about the way of it." He nodded, sat back, sniffed the coffee, and beamed at her. "And you know how to make a mean cup of coffee."

"I had to learn how to do that too," she admitted. "When I first arrived at Nan's house, I was pretty useless."

He chuckled. "I do remember Nan telling me about it, but you have learned since then, and that's what's important."

"I'm getting there." Then she remembered the cookies. She bolted to her feet again and raced inside, returning with a small plate. "I don't know if you've got a sweet tooth, but, if you like sugar in your coffee, maybe you'll like these. Nan helped me bake them."

He looked at the cookies in delight. "Ooh, cookies. If I'd known you had cookies, I would have come earlier."

She smiled at him. "I almost never have cookies. It's one of the few things that I'm just now learning to make. But Mack is in hospital, and I thought he would prefer cookies over flowers."

At that, Roger nodded immediately. "Any discerning male would. Cookies will never go wrong."

As he settled back, munching on the cookie, she asked,

"Now what can I do for you?"

"I just wanted to tell you firsthand what I came up with. Things can go missing in translation too often." And he took on a more serious air. "Used to work in the court system, years and years ago. And it was always pounded into us how important it was to have the truth be the truth and not embroidered in any way."

"No, I hear you there. That's something that I'm certainly learning, as I work on all these cold cases."

He gave another quick nod, eyed the cookies, and looked at her.

She smiled and nudged the plate closer. "Go ahead. They're best while they're fresh."

"Isn't that the truth?" And, with his fingers wiggling in delight, he carefully chose what looked like the biggest one on the plate.

"So tell me what you know."

"Lenny *Farsomething*." He pondered this a bit. "I think it's Farley, Fartherton—Farleigh? I don't remember. It's something like that. Anyway, Lenny is, was, a property developer, who ended up with a partner who was a little too shady for almost everybody's liking. But Lenny was enamored with him. Thought he was the best thing since sliced bread, and Lenny thought this guy could do no wrong. If there was a way to make a buck, this guy knew how, and Lenny was all over it. And unfortunately, in Lenny's case, he was persuaded by the mighty dollar at the bottom end. He started to love flashy cars, flashy women, high-end homes, and the lifestyle just sucked him in. Now this partner of his, he had a past down in Vancouver. I don't know what his name was. I probably did at the time."

Roger frowned, then continued. "However, that time's

long gone from my mind. Still, this guy was doing multiple deals down there as well. Now I don't think he was taking any of the materials from here and taking them to Vancouver. I think he was just involved in, you know, double-crossing people here that way.

"It finally came to a head when a big storm came, and a tree fell on a house, and, when the insurance company representative came to take a look, they realized what had happened. And, of course, that brought up this huge investigation. People got really angry, particularly those who had paid a lot of money for their high-end homes, only to find out it was half a home, as Lenny and his partner had essentially stripped out half of the supports and everything else that they could. So the homes were a danger to live in, but, more than that, the buyers were upset at being ripped off, and the city was upset because there are inspections for a reason, and these guys had found a way around it. And, of course, Lenny and his partner weren't the first ones to do something like this."

She stared at him, and he immediately shook his head.

"Oh no, whenever you find a way to make money illegally, and you have people prepared to do anything, they attract others so like-minded. In this case, I know there was an accident on one of the building sites, so it was a Workman's Compensation Board issue, back when WCB was brand-new. Therefore, there was an investigation because WCB felt they had to, you know, to make it look like they deserved a job." Roger gave an eye roll.

"And they found that not only were the construction practices subpar but so was the safety for the workmen. And I remember that somebody close to Mack was involved in the scheme. Maybe a close friend, a school friend, something like that maybe. I can't quite remember how it went. Anyway my understanding is Mack went to his bosses to open an investigation, and it all kind of spiraled from there. Now Mack didn't run the investigation, he wasn't even involved in all of it, but, in a way, he is kind of the person who started the police investigation."

"Right. So if anybody wanted to hold a grudge against him …"

Roger immediately nodded.

"Do you know what this Lenny person looks like?"

Roger frowned, as he thought about it. "Lenny was a small man. He would now be somewhere around"—he shrugged—"maybe fifty years old, something like that now. Could be a little bit older, but I don't think he would have been too-too much older." Roger stared off in the distance. "But you know the years just kind of go by, and you lose track of time, and, rumors being what they are, these could be completely false."

"No, I hear you there. So it is possible that this act of revenge was directed at Mack."

"I would think so, yes. I can't be sure though."

"No, I get it." She nodded, immediately letting him off the hook. "And the problem is, Mack's involved in any number of cases in that this Lenny or other people named Lenny could be associated with."

"Depends if any of these other names connect with that Lenny."

"Right."

Roger gave a sage nod. "That's basically what you're looking at now, is whether you can connect these other names to this Lenny that we're talking about, and, if so, then you know that you're on the right track."

"Exactly." She pondered that. "Any idea where Lenny is now?"

"No clue. I highly doubt he's local. He wasn't well thought of and kind of ended up running on a cloud of suspicion. Pretty sure he did a bit of jail time, but he might have done a plea bargain to give up his partner. I'm not sure. I seem to remember that the partner had it set up so that Lenny took a bigger fall than he did, and that's when they had a parting of the ways. Now rumor has it that Lenny's partner might have died in prison. You'll have to confirm that."

Doreen nodded. "And that's not unheard of either. So, these guys do a bunch of shady property deals. Somebody in Mack's world goes to him, asks for him to do an investigation. Mack starts the ball rolling and these guys know Mack started the ball rolling. They come back years later and take him out."

Roger looked at her in admiration. "You know what? That sounds about right."

"And it's full of holes," she said flatly.

He looked at her, shocked.

"Why now?" she questioned. "Why not fifteen years ago, when it came to light? And I know this guy was talking about *revenge best served cold*, but that's still a lot of years ago, and why shoot Mack? Why not the prosecutor who put him away? Or why not, you know, the judge who gave him however many years in jail or whatever it was? Why not his partner for that matter?"

"But maybe the shooter did kill all those other people already." Roger looked at her shrewdly. "Maybe Mack was just the last one. Maybe the shooter has a kill list."

She stared at him and slowly nodded. "We just don't

have enough information yet. We have lots of possibilities and not enough proof."

"Agreed." Roger rubbed his hands together. "So what do we do next?"

"It seems to me that we need to find a way to somehow connect these three names together," she muttered. She stared off in the distance. "Would you know anybody who might still be around today who would have more information?"

He pondered that, as he sipped his coffee. "Maybe," he muttered. "I know Lenny had a woman he was sweet on. And she had a daughter."

"A girlfriend's good. Particularly if she's still local?"

"I doubt it, but who knows?"

"Right, so there's all kinds of options here that we may or may not know about." She brought out her notepad. "So give me some names, and I'll run them down and see if anybody is around to talk to."

"Good enough."

"And who did Lenny stay with here in Kelowna?"

"His family."

"Family is even better," she said softly, that information making her smile. And, by the time he was done, she had a list of names to follow up on and people to go see. She beamed at him. "Now that was a lovely visit. You've given me lots to work with."

"Oh, good." He looked down and around, as if not sure what to do next.

"Do you want me to drive you home?"

"Nope, nope, nope." He hesitated. "But I wouldn't be averse to a little company."

At that, she realized he was hoping that she'd walk back

with him, whether it was because he wasn't sure he'd make it or if it would just make the trip a little easier. Either way she was happy to. "I'd love to, and so would the animals." She went inside, grabbed a leash, closed up her house, and called Mugs over. "We'll bring them all. Everybody here loves to go for walks."

He slowly got up, and she helped him down the steps to the deck.

"But, if you're not up to a walk, I don't want you to overdo it. I'm happy to drive you."

He laughed. "I'm overdoing it every day anyway. What's another day?"

She just smiled but watched in worry, as he made his way down the path. She paced her steps to match his.

As they walked along the river, he said, "We've had such lovely years here. Growing old is not something that you ever really think about, until, all of a sudden, it sidelines you, and you realize how many years have gone by. Don't wait." He looked at her carefully. "If there's something you want in life, go after it because, before you know it, all the opportunities are gone, and you're not even sure how it happened, but the time is ... is gone." He shook his head. "So, if you want to do something, if you want to be something, if you want to be with a person, even if you try and fail, it's still better to act than to wait. You don't want to look back and wonder, *What did I do all my life?*"

"I've certainly wondered about that myself recently. Nothing like studying all these cold cases—and the reasons why people do things and how it all comes apart—to make you take another look at your own life."

"And we all know Mack's sweet on you, so, if you've got any feelings for him, don't make the poor man wait. He almost died this time."

She winced at his not-very-hidden hint, and she muttered, "I was trying to get my divorce through first."

"That's pretty necessary too," he admitted, "but you know that you almost lost him this time."

"I know. I keep trying not to think about it."

"And he's been pretty upset every time you've been hurt. We all know it. And because we've all been there, we all understand just what it feels like. So make sure that you don't put off till tomorrow what you should be doing today."

She smiled at him. "Thanks for the advice."

He chuckled. "When I was your age, I would have said, *Thanks for the advice but no thanks.*"

"No, I'm not like that. I still have an awful lot in life left to learn. And just because it may not be the way I want to see things, it doesn't mean that it isn't just as important to hear the words of wisdom from everybody else around me and to learn from them too."

"If you do learn, you'd be one in a million."

She grinned. "Oh, I'm one in a million," she said in a cheeky tone. "I mean, come on. I'm Doreen."

At that, he burst out laughing. And when the chuckles finally died down, he murmured, "I'm glad I came. You're a good person."

"Thank you," she murmured. "And you're right. Some days we recognize the benefit and the value of others, and some days? Well, we all let it slide, thinking that there'll be time."

"And then the lesson, of course, is, there is no time, and you need to do it all now."

"And yet, if we do it all now, there's that pressure to get

done, there's that stress, that tension, to live up to expectations and to do and to be all those things. That doesn't sound like a healthy way to live either."

"I think that's why they said, *It's all about balance.* Which, you know, isn't something most of us are very good at."

"So true."

"I certainly wasn't when I worked in the court system. I saw my fair share of all those lovely criminals come in through the door. Sometimes we got it right. Sometimes we got it wrong. But I took comfort in the fact that every day we tried. Every day we did our best to make justice happen. And, whether we liked what happened or not, it was always one of those day-to-day things."

"I guess you saw lots of criminals, didn't you?"

"Lots. And lots of cases that we never got solved, never had a satisfactory conclusion to."

"I really would like to hear about those." He looked at her in surprise. She shrugged. "You probably knew the journalist Bridgeman Solomon, who was at Rosemoor. I inherited all the files he'd been working on and following over the years. I need to delve into all of them," she noted. "But again it takes time, and that's where I found some mention of the name Lenny and the developer information."

"Solomon was a good man. He used to get in trouble with law enforcement every once in a while, too. He would dig where they didn't want him to, but he was good at it. If you've got all his notes, I'm sure you'll find all kinds of cases to keep you busy over the next few years.

"A little too busy maybe." She chuckled. "Somewhere along the line I'm supposed to make a living." She pointed at Rosemoor up ahead.

Roger nodded. "The work you're doing on all those cold cases is important, but I get that you have bills to pay too. So you need a plan to do both. There's been nothing quite like doing these cases to realize just how much everybody else has a plan, and that plan doesn't include you. But in this case"— Roger smiled at her gently, as they walked toward the front door of Rosemoor—"Mack's life plan *does* include you, so make sure you don't waste any more time."

And, with that, he waved at her and walked up to the front door. She stood back, keeping the animals close, and watched as he crossed over the threshold into Rosemoor. And just as she was about to turn around and head back, she heard Nan calling her. Doreen looked over and smiled. "Hey, I just walked Roger home."

"Come in and have a cup of tea then."

"I probably even have coffee still warm at home." But she walked over to Nan's little patio, the animals racing ahead to greet her grandmother. Seeing her was always a highlight of their day.

Bending down to greet the animals, laughing at their antics, Nan finally managed to say, "It doesn't matter if you do or not," she muttered. She leaned forward and whispered, "Did Roger have anything useful?"

"He did, in a way, and I got a bunch of names to follow up on too. I'm digging into Lenny's history. Who he knew, family, friends. Who might have something to say about him, so I'll be on that this evening and tomorrow."

"Oh, good, and, if you want background on names, between us, we should have something to offer."

"I'll write them down in an email for you, or I'll give you a call later. I didn't bring my notepad with me."

"Of course not," she muttered. "But you know what? If

you don't want to stay and have tea, and you want to go home and get that notepad …"

"Meaning, I can go home and call you as soon as I get there with the names?" She narrowed her gaze at her grandmother suspiciously.

"Absolutely." Nan beamed. "We are anxious to help."

Doreen thought about that and nodded. "And, in this case, you're probably one of the best bets to getting information because it'll all be people who have been in town for at least the last fifteen years. So whoever has the most history here will likely have the most information to offer, but I can't be sure about that."

"Which is why you need to go get us the names," Nan repeated.

"Fine." Doreen tugged the animals back toward home. "Come on, guys. Nan wants to help find this person who attacked Mack."

At the word *Mack*, Mugs jumped and barked, his tail wagging like crazy.

"I'd love for Mack to come home to see us, Mugs," she muttered, as she headed toward the river again, "but Mack is stuck at the hospital."

And, with that sad fact, they slowly made their way back home again.

Chapter 15

Thursday Morning

DOREEN DID PHONE Nan later that evening, with a list of names—all family to this one Lenny. Nan immediately said, "I'm on it." And she took off running with the information.

Doreen didn't get a chance to tell her about the rest of her visit with Roger, but that was okay. Maybe it was enough for them to talk about for now. She had given Nan the names of Lenny's mother, sister, girlfriend at that time— even her grown daughter—and a niece.

But when Doreen got up the next morning, she wondered about the library. And the librarian—any of whom seemed to be long-term residents here in Kelowna. And, with that, Doreen quickly dressed, made coffee, and fed the animals. Then she poured herself a cup of coffee and had it while she sat down to review her notes, and then dashed to the library, sadly leaving her animals behind.

When she got inside, the librarian—the same one as last time—looked up and asked, "Now what?"

Doreen walked over and asked, "Do you know Lenny, the property developer?"

She sniffed. "I know about him. My grandfather was one of those who was tricked into buying one of his houses. It was quite a mess before he finally got it fixed."

"Did insurance cover it?"

The librarian nodded. "Yes."

"So it's one of those victimless crimes." Doreen nodded to herself, as that confirmed what she'd been thinking earlier.

The librarian stared at her in affront. "What do you mean, *victimless*? That was my grandfather."

"Sorry," Doreen immediately apologized. "I don't mean that he wasn't a victim. I mean *victimless* in that nobody is physically hurt from the crime, and, in this case, insurance pays out. And, as everybody hates insurance, they are quite happy to rip off insurance companies."

The librarian stared at her, nonplussed. "You know what? That makes sense. It's like stealing the little bits and pieces from a company—a pen here, a pad of paper there. People think it doesn't matter because the company will pay for it, and so nobody gets hurt by it. Unless you're the one who owns the company."

Doreen nodded and added, "And that's what these guys were doing, so it was easier for them to believe that they weren't hurting anybody." Then she pulled out the list of names that she had. "Do you know any of these people? It's Lenny's mother, his sister, his girlfriend back then, and a niece."

The librarian took the page from her hands, took a long look down at it, pulled her glasses farther down on her nose, and then looked up at Doreen. "I know of them. I don't *know* any of them."

"Okay, good enough. I was wondering how I might contact them."

She tapped the niece's name, Nettie Schumer. "She works downtown." The librarian thought about it for a moment. "I think she works for one of those spa places, doing the bookkeeping. She had bought it out and changed the name, if I remember correctly. She's his niece but not by blood. She was adopted."

"Bookkeeping? Somebody who's involved in this kind of crime?"

"I don't think she's involved in it though," the librarian replied, with a head shake. "I know she was pretty upset when her boyfriend got caught and ended up going to jail. They all worked for Lenny back then, and many of the younger crowd got caught up in the shenanigans and paid the price."

"I'm sure she was upset. Particularly if they were a solid couple and had future plans."

"She probably didn't know anything about the housing scheme. I mean, how would she?"

"That's the thing. I guess, unless you're actively involved in this business, she wouldn't know that that's what her boyfriend was doing."

"And she wasn't involved in all that at the time. I think she was doing spa work herself. But then she had a back injury and couldn't do the bending over and the physical work, so ended up getting her bookkeeping business set up instead. Yet she stayed in the spa industry because she already knows it."

"Now that makes perfect sense to me." Doreen quickly wrote down what the librarian had said. "I'll try to see if I can locate her."

"Try Nettie's Spa," she suggested. "I don't know that Lenny's mother's still alive. As I recall she had a heart attack not all that long ago." Then she shrugged. "But, when I say, *not all that long ago*, I mean that could have been ten years ago."

"Right," Doreen noted. "I could probably find out from the sister."

"Yeah. And the sister, she did get married, but I don't remember who her husband is." She pondered that, shook her head, and then quickly picked up her phone and called somebody. She put it on Speaker. "Hey, Elizabeth. Here's a question for you about the past, about Lenny and his girlfriend, Melissa, from the property mess some fifteen years back. Now Melissa has since died, I believe, but she had a grown daughter then. Do you remember Amanda something?"

"Yeah, she married Brad Greenwood and moved to Alberta."

"What about Lenny's sister, Celia?"

"That witch finally found a sucker to marry her," Elizabeth replied over the phone. "Figured she'd get the old man to the altar, but he was charged and found guilty before she could make it happen. So she went down a generation or two."

"Do you remember who she married?"

"Sure. She married Rodney, the old goat's grandson."

The librarian thanked Elizabeth and hung up, looking over at Doreen. "Rodney Bowman. I have to admit that does surprise me, but maybe it shouldn't. Celia's not the nicest of people and was always looking out for herself. There were lots of rumors she was sleeping with the old man, like Elizabeth said. She liked the money he threw in her direction."

At that, Doreen raised her eyebrows. "Now that is very helpful. You have no idea how helpful that is." And, with that, she dashed from the library.

Outside in her car she quickly phoned Mack. Yet, when she tried to get through, she couldn't, so she decided a quick hospital visit was in order. She got to the hospital and worked her way up to his room, but, when she got there, it was empty, as in *empty*-empty. As in there was no Mack, as in it was a freshly turned bed, and there was no sign of him.

Stunned, she looked up and down the hallway. Of course her heart immediately was afraid that something had happened to Mack, and he'd died. But she didn't dare go down that pathway. She caught the first person who she saw and asked about the room.

"Oh, Corporal Moreau left," the woman replied, with a smile. "He was arguing pretty fierce to leave, so the doctor finally decided, as long as he went home and stayed out of trouble, that he could be released."

"Perfect." Doreen grinned. "And I like that the doctor reinforced the fact that Mack had to stay out of trouble."

"And he wasn't allowed to go back to work for the rest of the week regardless. He was hollering pretty good about that too." The woman laughed. "So you can check with him at his home."

"Will do."

Grinning, she dashed back to her car. Only as she started driving home did she realize an uneasy truth. In all this time that she had spent with Mack, she knew all about his mom, and she'd met his brother, and she knew all about who Mack was as a person and the type of work he did and what he was like on the inside and so much more. Yet what she did not know—and it really concerned her at this point in time—is she had no clue where he lived.

She pondered all the conversations they'd had, but she didn't remember ever being invited to his place or having him say very much about where he lived or what he lived in.

He always came to her house; she never went to his.

Mack had always been a major part of her life, almost since her arrival in town, to be honest. So the fact that she didn't know where he lived was a conundrum that she didn't know how to get her mind wrapped around. It was an odd thing, and yet, at the same time, it was something that she knew she didn't dare even ask anybody else about. She got home, unlocked her door, stepped inside, and realized that none of the animals came racing toward her.

Worried, she ran to the kitchen, calling out, "Mugs? Where are you? Mugs? Goliath? Thaddeus? Where are you?"

She stepped into the kitchen, saw the back door was open, and cried out, "Oh no." She raced out onto the deck and stopped short. Her animals were there. They weren't alone. Matter of fact, they were sitting there quite comfortably with Mack. He was drinking coffee and lounging, for all the world like he owned the place. She stepped out and glared at him.

Mugs woofed and waddled over to greet her, but it was nothing like his normal exuberant greeting she would have expected if they'd been alone. Then again Mugs had likely already greeted Mack as his rescuer from their lonely prison. She bent down and hugged him. Then shot Mack a second look.

He raised a smug look at her. "Now what's that look for?"

"I was just at the hospital, looking for you."

His eyebrows shot up. "Then I guess you didn't get my message, did you?"

Frowning, she looked down at her phone and realized he'd texted her, while she was in the library.

"I was talking to the librarian," she said, raising both

hands in frustration. "So, no, I didn't get your text."

"The text was simple." And he quoted, "*I am being released. I'll see you in a little bit.* Imagine my dismay when I get a lift here and find you're not even home."

She glared at him. "But you made coffee."

"I did." He beamed. "Glad you stocked up."

"Hardly." Looking back at the pot, she groaned. "And you finished the coffee."

He nodded. "I have been waiting for a while."

She walked back into the kitchen, put on a pot, trying to calm down her mind.

"Not only was I shocked," she said, as she stepped back outside, "to get to the hospital and to find your bed empty— and honestly it looked like somebody had died in it—it took me a bit to find anybody to figure out just what had happened."

He looked at her and then nodded. "I didn't even think of that, but I guess you would immediately jump to the wrong conclusion, wouldn't you?"

"I tried not to," she muttered. "But it's a little hard when you go visit somebody, and you see that the hospital bed's empty. Besides, for all I knew, that gunman came back and made a second attempt."

He reached out a hand. "I'd give you a hug, but I can't move that fast."

She immediately raced to his side. "Are you okay? Maybe you should go back to the hospital."

"Not happening," he replied. "So don't even think about it."

She frowned at him, and he frowned right back. She sighed and sat down beside him. "I'm glad you're well enough to be released from the hospital. That was a little tricky."

"It was, and I'm fine. I'll be off work for a bit, and then I have lots of therapy to get through, but, according to the doctor, I missed out on a very ugly shoulder injury that could have lasted for years, being nothing but a big headache."

"Good. You have great timing being here now."

He looked at her with interest. "Why is that?"

"Because I found some more information. So maybe we'll get some answers finally."

"Like what kind of answers and what kind of information?" he asked suspiciously.

Chuckling, she told him what the librarian had said.

"Interesting," he muttered. "And you're right. I mean, the whistleblower was a friend of mine, Chuck, who started it all." Mack frowned at that. "Chuck moved to Vancouver a few years after that all happened."

"And how did Chuck happen to tell you?"

"He was cheap labor for these guys, trying to save up enough money to go to university. He was witness to their scheme. And I know he was pretty scared about getting involved, but he reported them anyway."

She waited a moment, then told him the rest. "With a group like that, I can't imagine telling on them. But, at the same time, hey, a lot of good came out of his tip. Plus we have connected two of the three names."

He looked at her. "What names?"

"The ones I told you about from Laura—Lenny and Bowman and Wilson. It's Rodney Bowman, and he married Celia Farleigh, Lenny's sister."

Mack stared at her in shock.

She nodded, a big grin on her face. "So take that."

Chapter 16

B Y THE TIME Nick came to pick up Mack at Doreen's place, Mack was looking a little unsteady.

She didn't waste any time and demanded that Nick take Mack straight home. "He needs to go to bed."

Nick took one look at Mack's face and nodded. "Let's get you home, big guy."

And, with them gone, Doreen walked back out to the deck, happy that Mack was out of hospital but worried that he'd gotten out too fast. But, of course, Mack was stubborn. She winced at that because she knew that he would say she was the stubborn one. The truth of the matter was, they were both pretty stubborn.

A little later she walked back into the kitchen, made herself a sandwich, all the while worrying about somebody following Mack home.

Uneasy that somebody, somewhere, would come back after Mack, she sent off a volley of emails to that extent, wondering if any kind of security could be set up for Mack at home and warning Nick to make sure he wasn't being followed. And then she texted Mack to stay away from windows. When she got a response back, telling her to calm down and that he knew what he was doing, she snorted.

"Sure, you do," she muttered. "That's why you got shot."

Sure, it wasn't fair. They'd been completely shanghaied by somebody lying in wait. And, at that, she tracked down the number for the niece's spa. Then she would try to call the sister. These were the places she needed to start.

"Nettie's Spa," bubbled out the cheerful voice.

"Hi, I'm looking for Nettie. Is she in?" Doreen asked.

"Just a moment." The call was put on hold, then an older-sounding woman answered.

Doreen quickly explained who she was.

"Oh, for Pete's sake. That was over and done with a long time ago."

"And it should have stayed there, except someone related to that original case has recently been shot."

Nettie cried out in horror. "Oh no, not again."

"Again?"

"Yeah, again. That was a nightmare back then for all of us. Now if you drag all this mess back up again, it will be a nightmare all over again."

Doreen winced. "I'm sorry, but this time around a cop has been shot."

"He likely deserved it," she snapped in a waspish tone. "My boyfriend at the time also went to jail for that mess. Left me alone and pregnant. I lost the baby and was angry for a very long time. Old Vaughn kept protesting his innocence, but he'd have done anything to save his skin. And his child."

Doreen froze at that. "So you were carrying Vaughn's child?"

"*Ewww*, that's disgusting. No, my boyfriend, Pauly, was

the father to my child. Pauly was always weak. I loved him to distraction, but he was weak. And he'd just do whatever Lenny and Vaughn Bowman and the others told him to. That's why he ended up going to jail. Stupid." Nettie's voice broke.

"I'm sorry. I didn't mean to upset you. But now that we have this new shooting, it will drag everything back up. There's no way not to."

Doreen asked several more questions, but Nettie was getting more and more morose as the conversation went on. Doreen thanked her for her time and hung up. Sometimes making these calls was harder on Doreen than the people she'd called. Determined to make the rest of the calls and aided with more details from Nettie, Doreen searched the internet for Lenny's old girlfriend, Melissa, but she had died of cancer ten years earlier. Doreen had better luck finding Melissa's daughter, Amanda. According to another quick search on the internet, Amanda married Brad Greenwood and resided in Alberta. Doreen called her but she had not much to offer in the way of assistance on this recent shooting or the previous construction scheme.

That left Lenny's sister, Celia. She was a local.

When Doreen called, she got no answer. Frowning at that, she quickly looked her up in the phone book and found Celia living about ten blocks away. Doreen hesitated because, as much as she would love the walk, and it would be good for her, she didn't really want to get stuck out too far away. But considering she had lots of daylight ahead of her, and that she hadn't done very much in the last few days, it would be good for her, she hopped up and grabbed Mugs's leash, and all the animals went crazy.

As if understanding that they would finally get a decent

walk, even Goliath raced toward her. Laughing at their antics and struggling to put on Mugs's leash because he wouldn't calm down, she finally got him buckled in, got Thaddeus onto her arm, and, with Goliath in his harness but not attached to the leash, she headed out the front door—setting the security alarm, and knowing Mack would be proud of her for that much alone.

She stepped out the back door, happy to not see Richard watching her. She and her crew thoroughly enjoyed the walk to the address she had plugged in to her phone's GPS. They went along the river, crossed over the roads, crossed over a bridge, and before she realized it, ten blocks wasn't very far at all. It was an odd section just on the other side of one of the main streets, called Lakeshore.

A block away was a big public park, rec center, and lots of fields, magnets for all the local sports teams to practice there. However, when it came to official games, there were those at home and those away, pretty much guaranteeing the parents a road trip at times.

It was a lovely area, not that it should surprise her. If these people were involved in nefarious dealings and making money, you would expect them to live in a nice area. Although they had to be careful, otherwise everybody would get suspicious.

Still Doreen had to remember that just because people might be suspicious didn't mean that they would do anything. Kind of like Richard, her neighbor. He was always suspicious of everything she did and was never really there to help out. Yet he'd been there to help in a big way at least once. She couldn't forget that. But, at the same time, he still hoped she would move somewhere else. Of course that wouldn't happen.

By the time she found the street she was looking for, she was surprised at the size of the houses. They were twice the size of hers. They weren't as fancy as the ones that she had seen up and down the river or down on the other side of Lakeshore, but these were still quite nice.

As she approached the address, she watched a young man come out, mid-teens maybe, slam the door shut, yelling, "He's not my father!",", to somebody inside the house. Then the teen added, "And how did he blow all the inheritance money?" before storming off. Doreen raised an eyebrow at that. As she kept walking forward, he stomped onto the sidewalk, brushed past her, and knocked into her slightly. She cried out. He turned and glared at her. She just looked at him.

"Good God," he snorted, "nothing but old ladies around here."

Doreen stiffened at that. "I don't know who you're calling old," she snapped. "Just because you're not old enough to clean behind your own ears, you don't have to yell at other people."

A woman from the doorway called out, "I'm so sorry. My son is young and impetuous. Teenagers, you know?"

For that, Doreen would have cheerfully called him angry and sullen, but, hey, she wanted this woman's cooperation, not to piss her off right away. Doreen gave a shrug. "He surprised me. He almost knocked me over," she murmured. She looked down at Mugs, who was looking up at her and rubbing up against her leg. "It's okay, buddy. I'm fine."

"Oh my," the woman said in surprise, staring at her motley crew. "Look at those animals. I have yet to see a cat wear a harness."

"He doesn't take to it all that well, but, if we go for long walks, then I do feel better if I have it, so I don't have to worry about him taking off on me."

The woman nodded. "Are you from around here?"

"I live over by the river. I'm exploring the local neighborhood."

"I've been here for years." She waved her hands. "Can't say I've done a whole lot of exploring."

"No? You don't like getting out and about?"

"I'm more of a homebody."

Doreen nodded. "Been there, done that myself. Sometimes it's just nice to explore a bit."

The woman shrugged. "Maybe, have a nice day." At that, she turned back inside, and Doreen took a couple steps past the woman, when she cried out, "Oh my."

Doreen turned and looked at her. "Sorry?"

"Is that a bird on your shoulder?"

Thaddeus had turned around on her shoulder and was poking through her hair and facing the back now.

"Oh." Doreen laughed. "Yes. This is Thaddeus."

The woman looked at her and then started to laugh. "You know what? I heard there was a crazy lady—" And she stopped, turned bright red, and quickly corrected herself. "A lady, in town here, who had a bird that went with her everywhere."

"Yeah, *crazy lady*, huh?" Doreen repeated, with a wry look.

"I'm so sorry. I didn't mean to insult you."

Between her and her son, they'd both done a good job of being rude, but again Doreen was trying to get along with Celia, or whoever this person was. So Doreen would have to think about this *crazy lady* comment later. "I don't think you're the only one to have thought it. I'm not exactly sure what I've ever done to deserve it though."

"I think having the animals is all that's required," the other woman said quickly. "Aren't you the one who solves all those crimes too?"

"Oh, every once in a while things stumble across my plate." Doreen laughed self-consciously. "Usually it's the police who get involved, not me."

The woman looked at her curiously. "Hah, that's funny."

"Why?"

"You'd think that the police would need your help right now. I heard a cop just got shot."

At that, Doreen raised her eyebrows in feigned surprise. "You know what? I did hear about that, and I do know the cop in charge, but I don't think they want me poking my nose into police business."

"Right," the other woman said, her voice hardening. "I don't have any love for the cops anyway. They made my life miserable years ago. And my mother's life. She died almost a decade ago now, still pining for old man Vaughn."

"Oh, I'm sorry, when these cases go sideways, it can get pretty ugly for everybody."

The woman nodded. "I didn't have anything to do with it either," she said indignantly. "And yet they jumped all over me and my brother."

"I don't know what the case was about, but, if you were innocent, then I would imagine that eventually they would all leave you alone." Mugs leaned up against her leg and whined. She reached a hand down to soothe him. He hated raised voices—yet wasn't showing any aggression so didn't sense any danger.

"Eventually, yes." Her face darkened. "Just not fast

enough. You end up having to live with it for a very long time, and it's not easy. You definitely start to feel very harassed about everything. Police brutality should not be allowed."

Doreen wanted to say something about harassment and brutality were miles apart but kept her mouth quiet. "I guess you really hate the cops now." She straightened, keeping an eye on Goliath who lay on the path, his tail twitching in hard jerky motions. Something was upsetting him too.

The other woman's face turned ugly. "Just the one."

"The one who got shot?" she asked curiously.

"Yeah, that one."

Thaddeus poked his head out from behind her hair and then immediately pulled back and hid. Obviously no one liked this conversation. Maybe they understood this woman's attitude toward Mack, who in their minds was family.

"At least I think it was him. Big guy. Way back then he was this idealistic cop. You know? Everybody should do right, and nobody could do any wrong, or he wanted to know about it." She snorted. "Like he was perfect, and we weren't."

"I've never been involved with the cops like that, but I can imagine how horrible it must have been."

"And once you're on the wrong side, they just hound you."

"That must've been a rough experience." Doreen stopped and frowned. "Hey, that wasn't to do with—let me think now." She stopped for a moment and pondered it. "Like a building company or something?"

The woman snorted. "Yeah. See? Even now memories are long. That was my husband's family. It had nothing to do with him and nothing to do with me."

Doreen looked at her. "It was something about property development or something. I don't even know what it was all about."

The other woman just looked at her. "Yeah, that's the thing. Nobody ever knows what it's all about," she said in a harsh tone. "They just assume the worst."

"No, you're right. I'm sorry. Obviously I've touched a nerve."

"Sure, but we're over that worst part anyway. I just don't want any of that to come around again. We'd never live it down a second time."

"I imagine, with this recent cop shooting, they'll have to look at all his old cases, to find likely suspects."

"It shouldn't have been his case to begin with, but he stuck his head where it didn't belong. Somebody told him something, and he believed it. The mess avalanched from there."

"Oh, ouch, that's the worst when you have snitches involved." Doreen gave a mock shudder, only to hear Mugs whine again. "It's okay, boy," she whispered. "We'll leave soon."

Celia laughed bitterly. "Everybody's a snitch when there's money involved. Even if you didn't do anything, they're out there to get you anyway."

"So you mean somebody got crucified, and they shouldn't have been?"

She nodded. "Yeah, that's what I mean. My father-in-law. His business was decimated over it all. He lost everything."

"And he had nothing to do with it?"

"Nope, he had nothing to do with it. He didn't know anything about it."

"Oh. Think about his life's work going down the tube and not being able to prove that he's innocent."

"That's the problem." The other woman glared at her. "He died protesting his innocence. He had to pay a ton of money, and he spent a year in jail, but he didn't do anything."

"Do you know who did?" Doreen asked curiously, hoping to keep Celia talking. Mugs had given up on pulling at the leash and was lying at her feet, waiting. In fact, her three animals were still. Too still. Likely waiting for everything to blow up.

"No, I always wondered," Celia muttered. "A lot of family members were involved, and, of course, everybody kept their mouths shut at that time because nobody wanted to go down the tube like my father-in-law did. I wasn't married into the family at the time. I've only been married to Rodney for the last what? Maybe thirteen, going on fourteen years." She stared into the distance, before turning her attention back to Doreen. "I wouldn't have touched him if he'd had anything to do with this, so I know he didn't."

At that, Doreen stared at her. "As long as you know for sure he didn't ..."

"Of course not." She sniffed. "He would never, ever get involved in something like that. He told me that he was innocent, and I believed him. I know how badly everybody suffered. So it wasn't hard to believe."

"I'm sorry. That is terrible. When things like that happen, everybody suffers."

"Exactly, and it's not fair," she cried out. "Vaughn was a good man."

"Sounds like you really cared about him."

"I did back then. He was always good to my mother and

me. I think he was kind of sweet on her, but, you know, the years go by. He worked hard, and you don't want to see that legacy go down the tube, but it sure did. And I blame the cop for that."

"How did the cop do it?" Doreen asked in astonishment. "Surely he was just investigating a crime."

"Sure. But somebody told him something, and he just kept digging and digging. My father-in-law was made to look like the guilty party. *If* there was any guilty party, ... I'm still not convinced about that either."

"What would it take to convince you? I mean, if there was a court case, and that didn't convince you, what would it take?"

"Nothing," she snapped, "because I'll never believe it." And, with that, she turned and walked into the house and slammed the door.

Confused, but with a lot to think about, Doreen slowly headed back home again.

Chapter 17

Friday Morning

WHEN DOREEN WOKE the next morning, still nothing was clear in her brain. She lay in bed, pondering the tidbits of information as she knew them. Obviously that Celia woman from yesterday with her rude son believed firmly that nobody in her Farleigh family or in her in-law Bowman family had done anything wrong. Or Celia was keen to keep repeating the lies until even she couldn't tell the truth from fiction.

Doreen needed to talk to Mack about it to make sure that he felt solid about whatever the case was and that he hadn't done anything wrong either. She considered that and then picked up the phone and called him. She checked her watch as it rang and realized that maybe it was too early. She quickly hung up and winced.

"*Great*, Doreen," she muttered. "You should have waited. The guy just got out of the hospital." As it was, her phone rang back immediately, and it was Mack. "I'm sorry," she cried out. "I didn't mean to wake you."

"You didn't wake me. I was already on the phone with the captain."

"Oh." She waited, but, when he didn't say anything, she asked, "Anything new?"

"No, nothing new. And apparently you've been sending off a volley of emails to everybody about making sure that I get protection."

She went quiet. "And?"

He sighed. "I can take care of myself. Besides, they know how to take care of me too. You know that, right?"

"But I don't know if they have the budget. I don't know whether they think you're a sitting duck or if they'll just let you flounder on your own," she snapped crossly. "So I had to make sure that they understood I wouldn't be happy if they didn't look after you."

He snickered. "I think you got your point across." He broke into big guffaws now. "I'm just not so sure that they appreciate your methodology."

"Whatever." She gave a wave of her hand. "They may not like it, but, if it got the job done, then that's fine."

"And what makes you think it got the job done?"

"I don't," she muttered, "but I'm hoping that somebody is looking after you." At that came a voice in the background. "Is that Nick?"

"Yes, it's Nick."

"Do you realize, when I left the hospital, after finding out you had been released, that I had no idea where you even lived? You're the one who's always over at my house and always drinking my coffee," she said, lowering the tone of her voice. "And I don't even know where you live."

There was a moment of silence on the other end. "Oh."

"Yeah, *oh.*" She gave a loud sniff. "That's all you have to say for yourself, *huh*?"

"What? Am I supposed to apologize or something?" he

asked, a note of laughter in his voice.

"I mean, it is kind of an odd thing to realize all of a sudden that I don't know anything about where you live, what your place looks like? You know there's a lot of personality in a place where someone lives. It would tell me a lot about you."

"You're welcome to come over," he said. "I have a bungalow not very far away. It's been mine for quite a few years, but I'm not here very much. So I can't say it's got a whole lot of personality, except some boxes, you know, a man-cave garage and all that good stuff."

"Wow, that sounds fun."

"Nope, not a whole lot," he said cheerfully, "but I certainly wasn't trying to hide where I live."

"It did make me wonder there for a moment. It also made me realize that I had never asked and, of course, then I felt bad."

"*You* felt bad?" he asked, humor rippling through his voice. "Why would you feel bad?"

"Because … it's probably, … you know, one of those things that you're supposed to ask about."

At that, he burst out laughing. "I don't know about things you're *supposed* to ask about." He chuckled. "I presume that the need just didn't come up. I'm not all that far away from you. It's about a ten-minute drive."

"Whereabouts?" she asked.

"North Kelowna. You're welcome to come for a visit if you want, particularly if you're bringing more cookies."

"I'm not bringing more cookies because they're gone," she snapped. "And you won't guilt me into trying to make them on my own either."

He burst out laughing. "Otherwise I would come up and

see you."

"Why? Are you out of coffee?"

After a moment of silence, he whispered, "Seriously?"

"Fine." She sighed. "I'm just teasing, but doing it badly, it seems."

"Good thing, and, yes, I am out of coffee." And he quickly hung up on her.

She groaned, as she stared down at her phone. "Of course you're out of coffee. Now I wonder about my own supply." She got up, dressed quickly, raced down to the kitchen to check on her coffee stash. She did have some, which was good; otherwise she would text Mack and tell him to pick up some. But then she realized that he shouldn't be driving.

She frowned, quickly pulled her phone back out, and texted him. **You can't drive.**

He responded immediately. **No, but my brother can.**

Which meant both of them were coming.

While pondering that, she opened the kitchen door for the animals, then put on coffee. With that done, she fed the animals, and looked around to see if she had anything to offer as a treat. She had a couple cookies that, instead of her eating them, she could give to them. Which she knew they would annihilate as soon as they got here. She stepped outside to sniff the fresh air.

She heard noises over at Richard's. Immediately a fat grin came on her face, and she crept over to the side yard and placed her ear against the fence. The voice continued for a little bit, but it was hard to decipher the words. It sounded like somebody was singing a lullaby. Then came complete silence, and, all of a sudden, she heard something against the fence by her ear, and Richard's head popped over the top of the fence. He glared down at her.

She immediately pulled a few weeds, stared up at him, and smiled. "Oh, hey. How're you doing, Richard?"

He cleared his throat. "It's you."

She stared at him, feigning astonishment. "Of course it's me," she said, with exaggerated patience. "It is my yard."

He snorted, looked around. "You haven't moved yet, *huh*?"

"Nope, not going to either. See? I've got this beautiful deck now. I have a beautiful pathway down to the river. Why would I move? Sorry, but you could be stuck with me forever."

At that, he just rolled his eyes. "Of course we are," he muttered. "And, of course, you're never quiet."

At that, she frowned. "I haven't made any noise all day. I don't know what you're going on about."

"Yeah, but you will get noisy. The day's young."

"And maybe today's your lucky day, and I won't make any." At that, she took a step back from the garden, looked down at the weeds, "I need to spend hours catching up on the weeds back here."

"Yeah, you do. Look at that mess."

"I haven't had a chance," she muttered.

"Why not?" he asked, looking at her as if he didn't believe her.

"For one, Mack's been shot. Or do you not remember?"

"How's he doing?"

"He's just been released from the hospital, although he shouldn't be driving."

"Of course not." Richard frowned and asked, "Why aren't you at his place?"

She raised both hands. "Because he says he's coming

over here right now."

"Ah, so then you will start making noise again." Richard shook his head in disgust.

"You make plenty of noise," she cried out, as he disappeared behind the fence.

"Yeah, but I'm allowed to," he grumped on the other side. And, with that, he went into his house and slammed the door.

Chapter 18

D OREEN SLOWLY PULLED a few more weeds, while she waited for the brothers Moreau to arrive. Finally wondering what was keeping them, she walked over to her deck. Just as she stepped onto the deck, Mugs started barking like crazy. It had to be Mack. And yet normally he didn't bark when it was Mack. But then again, if Mack wasn't driving, Mugs might not recognize Nick's vehicle.

She walked to the front of the house, and, sure enough, there was Nick's rental vehicle, a white SUV. At least it wasn't a green Jag. Every time she saw one on the street, it reminded her of her ex and made her heart slam against her chest. She watched from behind the screen door as they got out. As soon as Mack was out of the vehicle, she opened the screen door and let Mugs out. "No jumping," she admonished him.

Mugs immediately ignored her and jumped all over Mack.

Mack chuckled, squatted down, and, with his good hand, gently scratched the dog. When he looked up, he noted, "I see he listens just as well as you do."

"He's way better trained than I am," she announced.

At that, Nick burst out laughing. "I'm not saying anything to that. And, Mack, if you're smart, you won't either."

Mack shrugged. "I say stuff like that to her all the time. She gets mad, and then she gets over it."

"And maybe I won't this time," she growled at him.

He grinned and asked, "So is that coffee ready?"

"Of course it is," she muttered. "Did you bring any more coffee with you?"

"Do I need to?"

"Depends how long you're staying and how much coffee you're drinking," she said in a cheeky voice. "We'll run out eventually."

"Everything runs out eventually." He appeared completely unconcerned.

"In other words, you're planning on leaving before that happens."

"Absolutely." He chuckled. He straightened up and slowly walked toward her.

She assessed him closely. "You look like you've been through the wringer."

His eyebrows shot up. "Really? And here I think you look beautiful."

She flushed. "Oh no you don't. You should be at home in bed."

"That's not happening," he snapped. "So we're not going there."

"You've been injured. You need to take care of yourself."

"*Right*, and you need to stop texting everybody and asking who's on security detail to look after me."

"It's not a stupid question," she stated, glaring at him.

"Maybe not," he muttered, "but it's so irritating. I don't need security."

She crossed her arms and refused to budge from the top step.

But, in typical Mack fashion, he reached out and pulled her into his arms and gave her a gentle hug. "Still, I'm really grateful that you care. So thanks for letting everybody know."

She glared at him. "That's not why I'm doing it."

"Yes, it is." He gave her a look, then kissed her on the nose. "Now move." He stepped in her way, forcing her to back up.

She groaned and looked over at Nick, who was grinning madly. "Why are you grinning?" she cried out.

"Because I love seeing the two of you together. You two are great."

"This is great?" she asked in astonishment. "Did you hear him? He just ordered me to move, then totally ignored me."

"Yeah, I probably would too." Nick laughed at the expression on her face now.

She grumped at him and turned and headed back into the kitchen behind Mack. "He only comes here for my coffee. You know that." And then she heard Mack's cry of joy.

"And the cookies."

He'd already found the cookies. Coming into the kitchen, she noted, "That's all there is. So. if you eat them all, they're gone."

"Yeah. But there's no point in saving cookies because no one makes more cookies as long as there are still cookies in the house." She stared at him. He shrugged. "It's some kind of unwritten rule. As long as one cookie is left, cookies are still in the house. So everybody waits until they're gone before making more. So now," he added, "after today, they'll be gone. So you can turn around and bake some more."

"Not happening," she muttered.

She quickly poured coffee for the group, and, as she took it out to the deck, she heard Mack talking about the volunteer process and everything they'd gone through to get her that deck. As she set the coffee on the deck table, she looked over at Nick. "It was quite the day," she admitted. "The guys were incredibly generous with both their time and supplies."

Nick nodded at her and smiled. "Not everybody gets a chance to give back either. I'm sure that they appreciated the opportunity."

She frowned, but Nick shrugged.

"You've done a lot for this community, and a lot of people have been involved in your shenanigans." She glared at him. Nick held up a hand. "Just speaking the truth."

Her shoulders sagged. "Maybe. I've certainly met a lot of people I wouldn't have met any other way."

"And you've been hurt in many ways," Mack stated. "And not just by all the physical attacks on you but also hurt by society."

She studied him for a moment. "Maybe, but you know what? There's been a coming to terms with some of it too."

He looked at her and then nodded. "And that's a good thing. I know for a long time I worried because it upset you so to find out the way some people acted."

"It's hard. You find out that your view of humanity is very different than the reality."

He smiled. "And that's true. But you've been doing better than I thought."

She nodded, giving Mack a shy smile in return. "Thank you." She looked over at Nick. "It's been a challenge for both of us."

"You guys have come a long way though. I'm really pleased for you both."

At that, she wasn't so sure what to say, but she turned toward Mack. "Are you sure you should be out of the hospital?" He glared at her. She shrugged. "Okay. So, if it were me, how many times would you have asked me that question?"

He considered her for a second, then his shoulders slumped. "Probably just as many times."

"Right. So I'm allowed," she muttered. "You don't get to be defensive or pissed off."

He smiled at her. "Nope, and it shows me that you care, so I'm good."

She sighed. "Of course I care. Mugs missed you."

He shook his head, a quirk on his lips.

She gave him a smirk in return. "Drink the coffee. Before it goes cold."

He shook his head and looked over at his brother. "See what I have to put up with?"

Nick smiled at him. "Sounds to me like you've got the better part of the deal."

Mack nodded. "If she'd stay out of trouble, it would be fine," he muttered, then turned to her. "I'm surprised to see you home and not out sleuthing."

"No, I'm sorting through the sleuthing I've done. I'm not sure I should even update you on my progress." She waggled her eyebrows at him. "You tend to get cranky." At that, he hesitated, and she saw the muscle in his jaw twitching. "*Uh-oh.*" She looked over at his brother. "Do you see what's coming on?"

"Yep." Nick grinned. "Fireworks."

She shrugged, as she looked back at Mack. "You know I won't just sit here and do nothing. Somebody *shot you*," she snapped and glared at him indignantly. "And they shot you outside of my grandmother's place right in front of me. Do you think I don't feel guilty?"

"You don't have any reason to feel guilty," he snapped right back at her. "We've been over this."

She shook her head. "That's nice. You keep telling yourself that."

He groaned. "What did you find out?"

"Who said I found out anything?" She shrugged, speaking to Nick now. "Does it sound as if he wants to find out anything? No, it doesn't, does it? He just sounds cranky."

Nick's lips were twitching, and then he gave up the ghost and started to laugh uproariously. "Oh my, you two should be a comedy team."

At that, his brother gave him a quelling glance. "That is not even funny. Don't encourage her."

"She doesn't need any encouragement. You're right, Mack. But, oh my, you two are such fun."

"Not fun at all," he muttered, then glared at her. "Now will you tell me what you found out or not?"

"Not," she said promptly.

He put the coffee cup down very, very slowly.

She gave him an impudent grin before conceding. "Fine. Maybe I will."

"Maybe?" he asked in that same flat tone.

"Sure, maybe. As long as you stop looking at me like you're ready to yell at me. You know I don't like being yelled at."

He opened his mouth and then snapped it shut and continued to glare at her.

"Much better." She looked over at his brother. "See? He's trainable."

At that, poor Nick was in the act of taking a sip of coffee, and he ended up spewing it in all directions.

"Is the coffee that bad?" she cried out.

"No, no." And then he just laughed and laughed. "Oh, Lord. You two are quite something."

"No, we aren't. She is quite something, and at the top of that something list is *irritating.*"

She glared at Mack. "There you go. Back to insulting me again. You know I don't like that."

He sighed. "Fine, I apologize for insulting you."

She considered it and nodded. "Considering you're still suffering and you should probably be in the hospital, I'll accept the apology."

"I should *not* be in the hospital." He sighed. "Now, spill."

She shrugged. "Fine." And she slowly told them about the conversation with the local woman who was married to Rodney Bowman.

Mack nodded. "Celia."

"I do like that name." Doreen frowned. "How come you remember that name?"

"Because I remember the case."

"Ah, right. Celia said you would. She also said you were one of those young, snot-nosed, moral, know-it-all, fired-up cops and made her life miserable."

And he stared at her in astonishment. "Really?"

Doreen nodded. "Something along that line. She doesn't hold much love for you."

"I hardly spoke to her."

"I think she thought that you were fully responsible for

Vaughn, her father-in-law's, charges and for the loss of his family business and reputation. Apparently she had quite the relationship with him and really cared about the old man. He was devastated when this all went down, protesting his innocence right to the end."

Mack studied her for a long moment. "You know I didn't have much to do with that case, right?"

"Chances are you did what you normally do and went sleuthing and brought back the information and handed it over to the prosecutors, who either said they needed more information or they took it from there, and you moved on to any one of fifty zillion other cases."

He nodded slowly. "That is quite true."

She nodded. "The thing is, when people need a target, they don't really need facts nor to look very far. They remember the person they saw or associate with the questioning in all this, and you just became that target. And when she found out that you'd been shot, believe me. She wasn't sorry at all."

"And you didn't deck her?" Mack asked in amusement.

Doreen shrugged. "I wanted to say lots of things, but I was trying to get information from her. So, you know, she won't like me at the end of the day. Once again, my attempts to make friends in the community aren't working out so well."

He stared at her. "I don't even remember her clearly."

"And I think that would probably upset her as well because she remembers you."

Mack just shook his head and shrugged.

"So Celia is adamant that the Bowmans had nothing to do with her brother Lenny's construction con game. Which strikes me as odd, since Celia is choosing her husband's family over her own birth family. So do you remember Vaughn Bowman as being the partner-in-crime with Lenny Farleigh fifteen years ago?"

"Maybe. I wonder if I can get Darren to do a background check on him." He looked over at his brother. "Chuck was the whistleblower on this construction con." Meanwhile, he was on his phone, texting.

"I haven't heard from Chuck in years," Nick replied.

"Have you?" she asked Mack.

"Nope, sure haven't."

"Do you even know if he's alive?"

He stared at her. "No. I don't know that he's alive. I don't know that he's *not* alive. I have no reason to suspect either way."

"Maybe you should check it out."

"Why is that?" he asked, looking at her strangely.

"Because shooting at you is only of any value if somebody thinks that you have something serious to do with this. And how would anybody seriously think you had anything to do with this unless they were involved in the original crime, unless they got the information from Chuck, unless it was Chuck himself."

Mack's jaw slowly closed. "That's very logical. A lot of people were involved in that court case, not just me. I'm not the one who even investigated. I am the one who brought the investigation to my bosses though, so if they want to blame me for that ..." He shrugged.

"But that doesn't make any sense as to why they would have done something about this now. Why wait all these years?" Nick asked.

Doreen nodded in agreement. "I'm still trying to figure that out. Celia, outside of being a fount of animosity, didn't offer any helpful information."

"No, of course not. When you talk to angry, vengeful people like that, it's not the truth they're after. They just want their opinion validated."

"And there was definitely a sense of that with her too. Her family was *innocent*, and the cops *set up the old man*. So that's as far as I got. Although I do need confirmation that the old man died in prison. And, if so, Vaughn can't be involved in our current mess."

"Interesting." Nick looked at her, fascinated. "And this woman just openly talks to you?"

She nodded, noting Mack working his phone double time. She turned back to Nick. "It's kind of hard sometimes. You have to hit the right note to gain their sympathy or to piss them off enough that they spill, but I have found that generally, if I use sugar, I get a lot more from people."

"Of course. It is fascinating to see how you operate though."

"No, it's not," Mack snapped. "It's frustrating. People respond to her for some reason, and I know it's something that's confounded many of us at the police station."

"Honestly, I'm not sure that the captain likes me much. Did he ever tell you what happened at Rosemoor?"

At that, his lips twitched. "The captain didn't tell me, but I did hear from Darren. Apparently the gang down there listened to you just fine, but they completely ignored the captain."

"Yeah, that's about the way of it." She grinned. "Which honestly is just because they know me better."

"Sure, but they're supposed to have respect for the law."

"They do." She stared at him in astonishment. "But since when does that mean *listen to the captain?*"

He just stared at her, nonplussed. She looked over at Nick and caught his amused grin again. "What about you?" she asked Nick. "You got any news?"

"On Mack's case, no. Besides Mack would chew me out if I told you."

At that, she turned to face Mack. "Seriously? You have an update and won't share? You could save me a lot of time if you shared more information, you know?" He just glared at her. She shrugged. "Fine, be that way." She got up, grabbed her coffee cup, and went inside to retrieve the coffeepot. She filled up everybody's cup. "So how long are you off from work?"

"Too long," Mack muttered.

"They probably won't even let you investigate, will they?" she asked, catching sight of the look on his face, and then she chuckled. "That's why you're so cranky."

"According to you, I'm always cranky."

"You are, but it's something I'm learning to live with."

He shook his head "I am *not* cranky all the time."

She gave him a hard look. "Yeah, you are."

"I am not."

"Okay, whatever." She looked over at Nick. "I haven't been to your mother's garden in a couple days. How's it look?"

"Probably needs more weeding, but honestly I have no idea. I don't have anything to do with it."

"You're not a gardener?"

"Nope, not a gardener." He shook his head. "Although, if I move back into town, it might be something I learn."

"Why is that?"

"Apparently the gardens here are kind of deadly, and I might have to learn more about them just for self-preservation."

She stared at him, not sure if he was making fun of her or not, and then realized that he was quite serious. She nodded slowly. "You know what? It wouldn't be all that bad an idea. Some of the things that go on in this town are seriously bad news."

He smiled at her. "And yet you seem to be doing quite well for yourself."

"I don't think I'd go that far. Yet I am doing okay. It's Mack here who's in trouble. He's the one we'll have to help."

"Oh, I get it," Nick replied. "You need my assistance with my brother. And I would definitely help if I knew how, but it's not exactly my expertise."

"I always thought lawyers would be involved in everything."

He shook his head. "No, we tend to stick to our very clearly designated area, instead of getting caught up in other stuff."

"Hah," she muttered. "Not exactly what I expected."

"No, I'm sure it isn't. Sorry about that," he said, sounding anything but sorry. "It is the way of it."

"I'm getting help from Nan and the other Rosemoor residents. Otherwise I'm not seeing anybody else helping out." She looked over at Mack. "And honestly it's kind of strange not having you being active either."

"Yeah, me too. I'd do a lot to participate in this case."

"You know what you have to do then. Provide something that the captain can't justify keeping you out of it."

He shook his head and smiled at her. "It's not quite that easy."

She stared at him. "You know what? I suspect it's not all that difficult either. The captain just wants this solved and have it all go away. I'd like to think that that also means that he wants you to get better, but, you know, I'm not exactly sure where his priorities are."

"The captain's been a good friend and has treated me very well all these years." Mack smiled gently. "Don't worry. He cares about me."

She sniffed. "But he didn't provide any security for you, did he?"

"And I don't need security," he reminded her. "Besides, Darren was at the hospital providing security. Don't you have any more cookies?" His phone buzzed just then. He pulled it out and looked at the text.

"Nope, I don't." She stared at the empty plate. "Did you eat them all?"

"Nope, sure didn't," Mack said, but a guilty look was on his face.

She chuckled. "Considering it's my first cookie I've ever made, I'm glad that they went over well. It still won't get you off the hook though."

"Are you sure? Honestly it should."

"It won't," she muttered. "We need to get to the bottom of this, and we need to get there fast."

"Yeah, you got any idea how to do that?"

"No, not yet," she muttered. "And that's the problem. Normally I get a little bit information from you. I get a little bit from Nan, and right now I'm kind of stumped. I know what the case is all about, but we don't have enough to make an arrest."

"Imagine that," Mack teased in that dry tone. "And old man Vaughn did die in jail. One year after his incarceration."

"Thanks for the information although that just complicates things."

"Maybe, but Darren also said that Lenny dropped off the grid, right after his stint in prison. Darren's trying to locate him. If Lenny's still alive, he's in hiding. And I doubt he could hide for long here in Kelowna. My guess is he's down on the coast somewhere." Mack shook his head.

She frowned at him. "And I have to remember that you're not a cop right now. You're on medical leave."

"I am still a cop," he snapped.

"Sure, you are." She gave a wave of her hand. "And I get that you would be very upset if any of this were to go down, and you weren't a part of it."

"Yeah, you're not kidding. It's tough enough to sit on the sidelines as it is, but to know that everybody else is working this case—and yet I don't get to—is frustrating."

"They really will try and stop you?" she asked curiously.

"I wouldn't push it."

"*Hmm*," she muttered. "I would not want to be kept out of the loop."

"We're different people."

"Exactly. I know. I get that. I didn't realize I was such a rebel until I moved here. *Come to Kelowna, the place is peaceful,* my nan said. *Come to Kelowna, everybody is gentle and kind,* she said. *The lowest crime rate is in BC,* she said. You know why this city has the lowest crime rate?"

"No, but I'm sure you'll tell me," Mack admitted, with a sigh.

She glared at him. "Because you guys never solved any of these cold cases. Maybe that's why you guys didn't solve them—so that you could keep your low crime rate down."

He just stared at her, raising hands in disgust. "Seriously?"

"I don't know." She raised her hands, copying his move. "But I sure don't think Nan lied to me, at least not willingly. And, after that, everything else is off. I have no idea what is going on."

"Then why don't we get back to the topic at hand?" Nick suggested. "Let's see if we can come up with any theories about why and who might be involved in this."

"If we're going on the theory that this is all related," Doreen added, "first thing first is to find out if Chuck's alive. If he's okay, where is he? And has he done anything to restart this old investigation?"

"Why would you blame Chuck for restarting this?" Mack looked at her in confusion.

"It's not that I'm blaming Chuck. Still, what's his involvement if anything? Maybe he said something to somebody, or maybe he knew something back then and just spilled the beans now, and that started this whole mess rolling again. He's your friend. Call him."

"I'd love to," he admitted, "but I'm not sure I have his number." He looked over at his brother. "What about you? Do you have Chuck's number?"

She looked at Nick. "He was a friend of yours too?"

He nodded. "Yeah, he sure was. And I haven't seen him in a very long time either."

"Which is another reason for you guys to contact him. How do you know he hasn't been murdered?"

At that, Mack stared at her. "Do you have any reason for that comment?"

"Outside of the fact that we've been doing these kinds of cases for a very long time now, and murder has played prominently, why else would somebody try to kill you for a construction-related crime from more than fifteen years ago?"

"I don't know," he stated, staring at her, but the worry was starting to build on his face.

At that, his brother hopped up and pulled out his phone. "Let me try." And he walked a few steps away so that he could hear better and made a phone call.

She watched, as Nick walked away, and asked Mack, "Do you think Chuck has anything to do with this shooter of yours?"

"I would hope not," he muttered. "Chuck's always been a good guy in my world. He's the one who blew the whistle on this whole case some fifteen years ago. And it was tough on him at the time. He lost his job. A bunch of other people wouldn't hire him. Some people called him a snitch. It got ugly. He left for quite a while, although I did hear somewhere recently that he'd come back."

"And that could have been the trigger. Chuck returning to town. You know it doesn't take much."

Mack pondered that for a moment and then slowly nodded. "You could be right. It really doesn't take much, does it?"

She slowly shook her head. "And that's why I'm a little worried about him. Somebody could be extracting revenge on more people than just you."

At that, Nick came back to join them. "No answer."

"Call his sister Lisa," Mack suggested.

Startled, Nick immediately nodded. "Good idea." He walked a little bit away again.

"He was close with his sister?" Doreen asked Mack.

"Yep, very close, and she's good people too."

"When you start down this pathway, you need good people in your life. Otherwise it all goes off into the ditch, and you don't know what for."

He smiled at her. "Remember. Not everybody out there is a bad guy."

"Maybe not, but sometimes it makes you wonder."

Mack didn't say anything but watched his brother put away his phone and return to them. Nick said, his voice flat, "You won't believe this."

"Unfortunately I probably will." Mack sighed. "What have you got?"

"He was shot, four days ago. On Monday, the day before you were shot. And it doesn't look like Chuck'll make it."

Chapter 19

MACK STARTED A series of phone calls, and, by the time he was fired up and getting ready to leave, he looked over at Doreen. "Look. Now that you've been talking to Celia, I want you to watch out."

"Always." She looked at him suspiciously. "Where are you going?"

"Down to the station." She hopped to her feet. He held up a hand. "No, you're not coming. You're staying here, but I must go talk to the captain."

She nodded slowly. "I get that. I know that, to you, it may seem like I don't understand all this stuff, but I do."

"I know you understand way more than a lot of people do." He smiled in her direction. "I just don't want you to get involved at this stage."

"Okay, but you know that there's really no stage that I can get involved in that'll make you happy."

He burst out laughing. "That is the truth, but right now I need to talk to the captain." He looked over at his brother, who nodded.

"Yeah, I'll take you down."

"Now, stay out of trouble while I'm gone," Mack said

pointedly.

"Sure, but again you're forgetting who it is who brought you the information."

"No, I'm not forgetting. I'm trying to keep you safe."

She raised an eyebrow. "You mean, like I was with you?"

He sighed. "Okay, we'll both try to keep each other safe. That doesn't change very much."

"Sure, it does." She beamed. "I will let you leave and talk to the captain."

And, with that, he started out the door, and then he stopped and turned back to her. "That suspiciously sounded like something is on your mind."

"Not at all." She gave him her best innocent look. She looked down at Thaddeus, who was strutting back and forth on the top porch step. "Say, goodbye, Thaddeus."

"Say, goodbye, Thaddeus. Say, goodbye, Thaddeus."

Doreen beamed at Mack. "You stay safe and drive carefully," she ordered Nick.

"I will. We'll talk to you in a little bit."

She nodded. As they walked out, Mack called back, "You up for cooking dinner?"

"You up for supervising, or are you too injured for that too?"

"I am not too injured for anything." He glared at her.

"In that case, I'm up for making dinner."

"Good, we'll be back in a couple hours."

She nodded. And then, as they left, she realized they hadn't decided on what to eat. She quickly texted him. **What are we eating?**

He sent her a thumbs-up and a happy face emoji. **You choose.**

Trouble was, her choosing was one thing, but now she

was on the hook for feeding Nick too. She hesitated over all that for a long moment and then raced to her kitchen to see what she had available.

She found ground beef in her freezer, so took it out to defrost, and then checked the fridge for celery and her pantry for onions. With those locked down, she headed back to see if she had pasta. Spaghetti it was, and she even had a couple cans of tomatoes. In delight, she pulled everything out, set it on the counter, took a picture, and sent it to him. **Spaghetti?**

The response came back with another thumbs-up and then asked if she had garlic. She went back to the pantry, found two cloves, brought them out, and texted **Yes.**

Spaghetti it is then. You can do the prep work now, and we'll do the cooking when we get there, unless you're comfortable starting the sauce.

She thought about it and realized how many times she'd made the sauce and decided that she should sit down and at least chop the onions and the celery.

While she was doing that, she let her mind wander, trying to figure out who and what this Chuck guy was all about, because that seemed to be the root of this. As she worked, she texted Mack again. **What's Chuck's last name?**

When she didn't get an immediate answer, she immediately bugged him again. Finally he came back and gave her the name. **Chuck Howard.**

With that name, Doreen got the onions and celery sautéing in one pan and had the canned tomatoes simmering in another pot. Then she microwaved the meat just long enough to not brown the outside but to bring it to room temperature. She got a skillet hot with some oil and browned the meat, just enough to get rid of all the pink. Then she added the cooked hamburger meat and the chopped garlic to the tomatoes, topped off with the translucent onions and celery. She turned the burner to low and put a lid on the pot. She would wait to toss a fresh salad and to cook the pasta once the guys arrived. She didn't have any French bread. However, maybe Mack could make some magic happen with bread and more garlic.

She smiled at herself, very proud to get so much done on her own. And without a recipe even.

Doreen brought her laptop to the kitchen table and quickly searched for Chuck Howard. It didn't take long to come across articles out of Vancouver, saying that he had been shot. She quickly forwarded everything she found to Mack. And then Doreen searched for another name— Chuck's sister, Lisa Haywood, as mentioned in one of the articles. She knew that she could ask either Mack on Nick for Lisa's contact information, but that wouldn't help much because Doreen was pretty darn sure that both of the men would say, *Absolutely no way.* Of course they would. That's just what they lived for.

Smiling, she looked up Lisa Haywood in the Vancouver phone book and very quickly found six of them. And with that, she phoned the first couple, didn't find the one she wanted, but the fourth one rang true.

"Hey, I'm Doreen. A friend of Mack's," she murmured.

The woman paused. "As in Nick and Mack?"

"Yes." Doreen hesitated, "I don't know if Nick told you, but Mack was shot Tuesday evening, the day following Chuck getting shot."

The woman gasped in horror.

"He'll be okay," Doreen added quickly. "I just didn't know if any of this is related to what happened to your brother. And I wanted to call you and ask you personally."

"I have no idea." The woman sobbed. "My brother is in rough shape. It doesn't look good."

"I'm so sorry," she murmured. "Do you know what happened?"

"No, not … not really. The cops are investigating."

"Right, of course they are," Doreen agreed. "Look. There's been some suggestion that it might go back to the case some fifteen years ago, where Chuck contacted Mack about the property development crime he reported happening at his job."

Lisa gasped. "You know what? That did cross my mind. It just never occurred to me that they would go after Mack too."

"I don't know for sure that it's the same shooter, but Mack and I are friends, and we worked on a lot of cold cases," she improvised. "And I know he'd be really angry if he found out I was talking to you, but I just … I find it hard to leave it, knowing someone could make a second attempt on Mack's life."

"No, I hear you. If I had any way to find who shot my brother," she said, "believe me. I'd be all over it too."

"Do you have any idea who would have done this? Did Chuck have any enemies, or was he worried about anybody in his circle of friends? Did he think he was being followed? Were there any signs that something like this could happen?"

"No. At least not as far as I know. He didn't tell me if there were any problems, and I would like to think that he would have. I just … I don't know."

Lisa sounded so grief-stricken that Doreen hated to even push for more information. "If you do think of anything, if you could let me know, I'd really appreciate it," Doreen murmured. "And, if I hear anything that might connect this to your brother's case, I'll let you know."

"I'd appreciate that too," Lisa said gratefully. "Sometimes I think we have to do our own investigations because the police are so slow."

"The problem is the police just have so many cases. They get like forty-eight hours to work on this one case, and, if nothing breaks, well, they're off onto the next one."

"And how fair is that?" Lisa cried out. "It's just terrible. Anyway, obviously you know my name and number, so if you hear anything, please let me know."

"Will do. And, by the way, I understand the scene of the crime was close to a local bar. So was Chuck at the pub with anybody?"

"He met a friend there." Lisa's tone of voice changed. "Chuck met Dante."

"Okay. Do you have a number for Dante or a last name?"

"I have both. Hang on a sec." She rummaged through something for a moment on the other end of the phone and then said, "Here it is. It's Dante LaPointe. They've been friends for a long time."

"As in so maybe they worked together in the same construction industry way back then?"

"You know what? I think so. They probably went that far back. You don't think Dante's involved, do you?"

"No, I just wonder if maybe he saw anybody, if he was out there talking to Chuck, or who knows what Dante might know. I've found doing all these investigations that the more people think they know, it really means the less they know. On the flip side, people who seemingly know nothing just don't understand that usually they know something important. Someone just needs to point it out to them."

"I sure hope that's the case right now. I would do a lot to make sure that my brother survives this," Lisa murmured. "It just seems so unfair that somebody who has done as much as Chuck has to turn his life around would be in this position now."

"Do you want to clarify what that means?" Doreen asked curiously. "Mack hasn't filled me in, outside of the fact that Chuck's the one who told him about the construction scheme that had gone on all those years ago."

"Yeah, that's exactly what happened. He was the whistleblower there, but Lenny fired him. Chuck couldn't get a job for forever after that. Finally Chuck landed another construction job, but soon also got into trouble with that boss. I guess Chuck was at that stage where he was like, *Everybody else was cheating and lying so, why shouldn't I steal a little bit*," she explained. "And so he ended up losing his job, plus getting beaten up pretty good from this ordeal. He reached out to some underworld types to get himself out of debt, and that gave him enough money to run but he also got caught. So Chuck did two years in jail. And then he got out and started retraining, trying to get his life together." Lisa started crying again. "And he worked so hard at it. It's just not fair."

At that, Doreen stared down at the phone. "Any chance one of his jail buddies shot him?"

"I don't think he had any," Lisa said bluntly. "He was really angry at himself, figured he probably should have talked to Mack about giving him a hand to get out of prison, and, for all I know, Chuck did speak to Mack. Chuck was pretty worked up over it all."

"As I understand things, Mack, as a cop, has very strict

rules to follow. So, if Chuck were guilty, and it seems he was guilty, there's just not a whole lot Mack can do in those cases."

"No, and that I think is why Chuck didn't really want to talk to him. He also was pretty embarrassed because, after everything Chuck had done to clean up his life, he was the one who had fallen prey to the temptation."

"And that's always tough too, isn't it? We want our family to do what's right, but sometimes what's right ends up feeling very much like it's wrong."

"Exactly." Lisa sniffed into the phone. "I really hope that Mack'll be okay."

"He will. Yet I'm worried somebody might come back and try to finish the job."

Lisa gasped on the other end. "That would be absolutely terrible."

"Yes, it would," Doreen agreed. "As you can tell, I really care about him."

"Yes, yes, and with good reason. He's a good man. I know he was there for my brother the whole time through this ordeal, so, if these two shootings are connected, that kind of makes sense."

"It does. I mean, Mack told me that he wasn't involved too much in the investigation part because he was still a rookie cop back then, and it wasn't his department, but ..."

"No, it wasn't, but he gave my brother a lot of moral support, and that kind of support matters. Mack's a good man. And so we really want to make sure that, if people are there for us, that we're there for them."

Not long afterward, Doreen disconnected the call and sat here for a long time, thinking about what Lisa had said, because she was right. You did want to support those who were there for you and particularly for that long-term support, and that was just like Mack. He'd been there every step of the way for Doreen. And, with that, she was more determined than ever to find Mack's shooter.

She could now smell the sauce, and she headed to the pot, trying to figure out just what all this meant about Mack's case, as she stirred the mixture. Almost immediately she heard Mugs barking in the front room. She walked out to the living room and looked at him. "What's the matter, buddy?"

He started barking at the front door and wouldn't stop. With her nerves a little bit on edge, she looked out but couldn't see anything. Still Mugs didn't caterwaul for nothing.

"Okay, so now you've got my attention, but I'm just not sure what's going on. What's the matter?"

He barked and barked again, but she wouldn't open the door. Matter of fact, she returned to the kitchen and turned on the alarm. This time something inside her said, *Don't do it, Doreen. Stay quiet. Stay in control, and do not open that door.*

When a hard knock came on the front door, she stared at it, wishing she had a peephole. But she didn't, and she wasn't sure what to do. When the doorbell rang and then somebody tried the handle, she winced at that. Of course Mugs went absolutely chaotic crazy as soon as somebody tried that door. She wished she could calm him down, but she wouldn't do that either.

She waited, but there was no repeat ring. She remained cautious, and then darn if she didn't hear footsteps going around to the back. She gasped and ran to the kitchen door, managing to lock it just before a hand reached out for it, but yet obviously her uninvited guest had heard the *click*.

And then started slamming on the back door. A man yelled, "Open the door or else."

But she didn't recognize the person, and she sure didn't recognize that voice. She quickly texted Mack. **Somebody's trying to get into the house.**

Her phone rang immediately.

"What do you mean, somebody's trying to get into the house?" he cried out.

She held up the phone so he heard whoever it was pounding on the back door. "You hear him?"

"Yeah, I'm on the way. Phone the cops."

She stared down at her phone and winced because calling the cops would delay everything in her world quite a bit, including lunch. But, if Mack said so, she didn't really have a whole lot of options. She quickly phoned 9-1-1 and explained what the scenario was. She held up the phone again, so that the dispatch operator heard the man banging on the door too.

"Stay inside. Keep the doors locked."

"Oh, I am, but this guy is pissed."

"Yeah, he sure is," she muttered. "We've got a unit on the way."

"Good. I don't know if he'll get here fast enough though."

"What do you mean?"

"I think he's starting to break down the door."

And, sure enough, as she stared in shock, she watched as the door shook really hard at the hinges. "I think he'll bust it open," she cried out.

In the background she heard the man roaring, "Let me in, you crazy woman."

"Can you run out the front door?" the dispatch operator asked Doreen.

"I might, but there's no guarantee he won't come racing around to the front and catch me there either."

"Hold tight. Unit's on its way."

She could tell that, for the dispatch operator, that mantra was supposedly good enough, but Doreen wanted to tell her that it wasn't even close to good enough. Whoever this guy was, he had an agenda. She hung up the phone, walked over to the kitchen door, and yelled, "What do you want?"

The man went quiet for a moment. "Let me in."

"Yeah, like that's happening," she snorted. "You're not getting in, and I've called the cops."

"The cops won't save you."

"Why are you mad at me?"

"You came and talked to my wife yesterday."

Doreen stared at the door. "You're Rodney Bowman?"

An ugly snort came from the other side of her back door. "Look at that. She knows who I am."

"Yeah, I mean, Celia told me who she was. And I guess that was your son, who almost knocked me down on the sidewalk then?"

"Stepson," he stated, swearing at the door. "Thinks he's top dog."

"He was pretty pissed off too, so, for all I know, your whole family is loopy and has anger issues."

"We're not loopy," he roared. "And I sure don't like people insulting my family like that."

"Maybe not, but you're the one pounding on my door like a crazy man."

He stopped for a moment, then said, his voice low and ugly, "If you don't open this door, I'll come back."

She snorted. "I don't know what kind of world you live in where that kind of a threat will get you inside my door because obviously no way I'm opening this door to some angry, crazy person. I don't know what you want, but you can leave at any time."

"If you don't stop asking questions, you can bet I won't be stopping what I'm doing. You just remember. I know where you live."

"Yeah," she snapped in a moment of bravado. "Remember. I know where you live too."

Chapter 20

"YOU DID WHAT?" Mack roared at Doreen for the third—or was it the fourth?—time. "Please tell me that you didn't tell him that."

"What was I supposed to say?" she asked, staring at him. "He was threatening me."

"Yeah, he was threatening you. In most cases people would try very hard not to piss off somebody like that."

"No point in trying to *not* piss him off. He was already pissed off. What did you want me to do?"

"I don't know. How about stay quiet until the police arrived?" he snapped, glaring at her.

"Did you expect him to stick around while the sirens were racing up here?" she asked in astonishment. "Of course he didn't hang around."

"Yeah, well, just imagine if he had though." Mack rolled his eyes.

She glared at him, hugging Goliath close in her arms. "And why are you angry at me?"

He opened his jaw and then slowly snapped it shut. "Good God," he said, "I can't even …"

"No, and you shouldn't," she scolded him immediately.

"You're supposed to be at the hospital."

He roared, "I am *not* supposed to be at the hospital."

"You'll have a heart attack if you keep this up. You know how crazy you get around me."

He sank back into the closest chair and looked over at the cops.

She knew one of them but didn't recognize the other one. But she smiled and gave him a cheerful wave. "Hi, Arnold. I really appreciate you guys coming. That guy was pretty scary."

The one guy looked at her, fascinated. Arnold just smirked. "Yeah, so scary, you probably terrorized him."

"Not yet," she confessed. "I was kind of waiting for Mack to do that."

At that, Arnold laughed. "And Mack's likely to terrorize you now."

"I don't know why he's upset," she snapped. "I'm just trying to keep him safe."

"You've even texted me," Arnold noted gently, "asking about security for Mack."

At that, Mack turned ever-so-slowly and glared at her. She threw up her hands. "If it was *me*, what would you do?"

He opened his mouth, but his brother tapped him on the shoulder. "She has a point."

Mack snapped his mouth shut and turned to now glare at his brother.

His brother shrugged. "You know that, if we're being honest, she's right."

"I won't be that honest," Mack bit off.

"See? See? That's the problem. You want me to be honest, but you won't be honest," Doreen cried out. "How fair is that?"

Mack slowly shook his head. "Oh my God. Every time I think we're getting somewhere, you do something like that."

"What? I wasn't supposed to talk to Rodney? To find out what he wanted? He was breaking down my door."

"Talking to him is one thing. Riling him up to the point where he damaged the door like he did? That's a completely different thing." He paused, then added, "You know you need a new door now, right?"

She stared at him. "*Uh-oh.*"

"Yeah, *uh-oh.*" He gave her a clipped nod. "There's a price tag attached to those things."

She glared at him. "Then *he* should pay."

"Oh, yeah, great." Mack glared at her. "And how do you expect to make him pay?"

"I'll go tell him." She marched toward the doorway.

Mack immediately groaned, reached out, snagged her hand. "You're not going anywhere."

"He ruined my door," she cried out. "That costs money. I don't have any money. Remember?"

"Yeah? Remember that part about not pissing people off?"

She glared at him. "I had full rights today. This was my house. I was safe and sound and locked up in my own home. I shouldn't have to pay for a door that somebody else busted."

He just stared at her. Doreen looked over at the cops for confirmation, "Right?"

Immediately Arnold nodded. "You know something? I think that's quite fair, and that's why people have something called insurance."

She sniffed. "I know Nan put insurance on this place, but I don't think it covers idiots kicking in doors."

"You're just lucky that we all arrived when we did, and so he didn't make it all the way into the house," Arnold snapped.

She glared at him now. He just hitched up his belt over his rather large girth and grinned. Slowly her shoulders slumped. "I was just trying to make spaghetti," she wailed.

At that, Nick lifted his head, sniffed the air, a look of hope on his face. "I wondered at that aroma when we arrived. It's spaghetti sauce." He looked at her in delight. "Man, you will still feed us, won't you?"

"I was going to, before your brother got to be so irritating."

Nick immediately got a woebegone look on his face. "Does this mean you're not feeding us then?"

"Of course I'll feed you. It looks like it'll be dinner, not lunch though," Doreen sighed. "However, you have to keep your brother back."

He studied her, and his lips twitched. "Hold him back so he doesn't attack you?"

"Mack would never hurt me." She glared at Nick. "Why would you say that?"

At that, Mack just groaned. "Don't even bother getting into a conversation with her. It never works out well."

"You don't know that." In a small voice, she asked, "I'm not difficult, am I?" And she looked at all the other men in the vicinity, but nobody jumped up to defend her. At that, she realized that they wouldn't. She sniffed. "Fine. You guys do what you must do. I'm going back to my spaghetti sauce."

And, with that, she took one last look at her door, which upset her all over again. And she had no clue how to fix it or what would be required. As she sniffled half in frustration and half in rage, Mack stepped up to take a closer look at the damage. She moaned. "I suppose I needed a new door from the beginning anyway."

"It was one of the things that we thought needed to be fixed," Mack muttered, "but it wasn't very high on the list."

"Yeah? Guess what? It just moved to the top of the list."

Chapter 21

Saturday Morning

THE NEXT MORNING Doreen woke, still feeling the frustration rolling through her. Or maybe the heaviness on her chest was due to a sound-asleep Goliath. Mugs was stretched along the right side of her body, and Thaddeus was sound asleep on his roost.

Cozy, tucked under the covers, Doreen thought about the previous evening. The spaghetti had turned out wonderful, although Mack had not relented very easily last night. He'd been pretty upset all through dinner. She understood how he felt because, well, apparently that's how he felt every time she went off doing something crazy like that. But, at the same time, it wasn't really her fault. What was she supposed to do when a madman tried to kick down her door? Hide inside like a mouse? She'd been a mouse too much of her life. She wouldn't be a mouse anymore if she didn't have to. Was it the wisest thing to do? No, probably not, and maybe Mack had been justified in being upset with her for goading the madman, but, at the same time, surely she didn't have to take that attitude from Mack. It just felt like she was always on the wrong end of the stick.

If she fought back, she shouldn't. And, if she didn't fight back, she should have.

Trying to get out of that depressing mind-set, she had a quick shower, dressed, then walked downstairs and outside to the deck. Walking back inside, she fed the animals and put on coffee. With her first cup, she headed outside, sighed glumly on her deck—her beautiful deck that Mack had arranged. Her hand gently stroked the wood railing that all the men had pulled together to create to make sure she had a safe deck and groaned at the sight of her faithful dog.

"Mugs." He woofed at her and flopped down beside her. "I guess I have to apologize again, *huh?*"

He just woofed yet again. She reached over, gave him a big hug, and reclined half on top of him. "I'm really glad that you guys are easy. It's kind of hard dealing with people."

She didn't want to make too much of herself again, but, boy oh boy, sometimes it was just not easy being her. She didn't think she was difficult to get along with, but, according to these guys, well, she was. She sat here for a long time, thinking about it, and then picked up her phone and texted Mack. **I'm sorry.**

Feeling better, even though she wasn't fully in the wrong, yet she could have handled Rodney differently, and she could have handled Mack differently. But it seemed like everything was all new. None of her skills from before fit anymore because she wasn't the same person wielding them. She didn't seem to have a diplomatic bone in her body anymore. All she wanted was to make sure that she could get the answers to questions that really, in some ways, weren't even her problem.

And she hadn't even told Mack that she'd phoned Chuck's sister, Lisa. That wouldn't go over well either.

When her phone buzzed, she looked down, and there was a heart. Immediately she gave a happy sigh, and it was followed quickly by his text.

I'm sorry too.

She stared down at it and realized that was one of the things about Mack. She could mess up, and she did regularly, and still they could come together the next day and apologize. Mack messed up, and he did regularly, and still they could come together the next day and apologize. That said a lot. He might not understand how she was still struggling with this sense of right and wrong, this sense of why he could do what he could do and she couldn't, and why she felt the need to always be in the way or doing her own thing.

It seemed she'd spent so many years not being able to do anything her way that now it was just this big challenge to not force herself into Mack's world. And yet whenever it came to his world, it seemed to be the one thing that she wanted to do. And, of course, that wasn't fair to him either.

Her husband would have yelled that she wasn't allowed to go there. There had been a couple times when Mathew had done that. But she had learned at that point that getting beat and face-smacked and belittled and demoralized was just not one of the things that she wanted to remember. Not now. Especially when she realized that Mack was as opposite to Mathew as anybody could get. When the phone rang not too long afterward, she expected it to be Mack, but instead it was Nan. She smiled down at the phone. "Hey, Nan. How're you doing?"

"Better than you are, apparently. Are you all right?"

"I'm fine," she murmured. "It was a rough day yesterday."

"I'd say so," Nan agreed. "I just heard from the grapevine."

"And, of course, I got in trouble with Mack again."

"Ah, don't worry about it," Nan said, chuckling. "He'll forgive you."

"He always has. I just wonder if there's a limit to that forgiveness."

"No. There really isn't, not when he cares so much."

"But I keep pushing his patience."

"And, if you don't, no one will, and Mack needs somebody like you. It's too easy to become entrenched in doing the work he feels so emboldened to do, and there's nothing else in his life. He needs somebody like you to make him smile, to make him laugh, to make him cry," Nan said gently. "Even if you don't feel like it has value, I can tell you—as somebody very much older and more experienced— that you bring him a lot of value. Often we forget about our humanity. We forget to stop and to smell the roses, and we forget there's something other than our duty. And Mack is very duty-bound. He will always try to do the right thing. He will always try to do what you need him to do. And so, it's important, when you feel you need to do something, that you do it."

"I just feel like sometimes I'm disappointing him."

"Then you disappoint him," Nan stated firmly. "You still are in a stage of life where you're trying to figure out who you are, what you want, what you can do. And I think it's very important, especially right now, that you be *you*."

Doreen smiled. "In your world, I should always be me."

"Yes, I agree with that in some ways, but I also understand that it's easy to allow you to be you without any conscience, and that's not what we want. We still want you to be very conscious of everybody else around you and all the things that are important to you. It's also a matter of being you and being free enough to do what you believe in. And, in this case, you're already there. You already believe in Mack and what he's doing. You already believe in what you're doing. We don't want you to change. We just want you to stay safe."

"And what about Mack being safe?" Doreen cried out. "I contacted all kinds of people to make sure that they have security set up for him."

Nan stopped. "Protect him from what?" she asked cautiously.

"Nan, somebody tried to kill him. What'll stop this gunman from coming back and trying again?"

"Oh my." Nan hesitated. "You know what? That's one of the things that I hadn't considered, and obviously I should have."

"No, it's … it's fine. You didn't have to consider it. I considered it, and I contacted everybody. Mack didn't like that."

Nan chuckled. "Of course not. I mean, basically you were questioning his ability to look after himself, and that's something men have trouble with."

"But he got shot in the first place," she said in a reasonable tone. "So, of course I'll have to question that."

"Of course you are." Nan giggled. "Good thing Mack is a self-secure male. Otherwise his ego would take a hit. However, you shouldn't be upset when he gets a little irate because of it."

"Maybe," she muttered, "but I still didn't think it was that big a deal."

"No, you wouldn't. You weren't questioning his abilities. You were hyperfocused on keeping him safe from an active assailant. In case you ever doubt it, you need to know that Mack really loves you. He's exhibited oodles of patience with you, and he's been very, very good for you, but, at the same time, you've also been very good for him. So give him a little bit of space, let him know that you care, try not to choke him with all this, and it'll work out."

"I think we kind of worked out some of it. At least he's talking to me today."

"That's good," Nan said, chuckling, "because that's important too."

"It is," Doreen agreed. "It really is."

"Anyway, just a word of warning. Remember. Love makes us crazy."

"It makes *him* crazy." Doreen sighed. "I'm not crazy."

"No, of course not." Nan laughed. "Remember to add in tolerance and patience."

"Right, I'm working on it."

"Have a lovely day," Nan said, and she rang off.

Chapter 22

BY LATER THAT afternoon Doreen was bored, frustrated, and fed up again. This was all going nowhere. Contemplating what she'd already learned and seen so far, she realized that she'd forgotten to ask Laura one important thing. She quickly picked up her phone and dialed the woman who worked at Rosemoor and who spoke to the gunman. When Laura answered, her voice distracted, Doreen immediately apologized. "I'm so sorry. It's Doreen. I forgot to ask if you caught any of the license plate number on the shooter's car." Laura took a moment, probably figuring out who was on the end of the phone.

"Oh my, that Doreen. You know what? As I was standing there that night, waiting for him and his phone call to end, I did notice that he had a big dent on the back left-hand side of the vehicle. As I walked away, I did see an *L* and an *M* in the license plate."

"An *L* and an *M*," Doreen muttered, shaking her head at how belated this information was. Doreen only had herself to blame for not asking earlier. She could blame her worry about Mack for that.

"Yeah." Laura giggled. "I saw the letters and immediately

my mind said, *Love Mack*." She laughed. "It's a trick I've always used to memorize words. Also the license plate didn't look like it was attached properly. It was hanging sideways a bit."

"Right, so it might not even have been the right license plate for the car." She didn't dare mention the *L* and *M* mnemonic to Nan, but, boy, would she have fun telling Mack.

"And that's possible too. I ... I don't know."

"And, of course, you didn't remember anything else about that interaction, did you?"

"Honestly, no," she replied apologetically. "I spoke to the cops, but I didn't have any other information to give them." She hesitated and then asked, "How is Mack doing?"

"He's been released from the hospital," Doreen replied, grateful to say those words.

"Oh, that's lovely," Laura cried out. "I'm so happy to hear that. He is a lovely man."

Soon they hung up, and Doreen quickly sent the information to Mack, minus Laura's memory trick.

He called Doreen almost immediately. "Why didn't you tell the cops that?"

"Maybe the cops already know. Maybe the cops just didn't tell you about it. Maybe they're keeping you out of the investigation so you don't go all hothead on them."

A moment of silence passed on the other end. "Hothead?" he murmured in a neutral tone.

"Yes." She grinned. "But then I understand it. I do know what it's like to be attacked."

"Yeah, you think?" he muttered. "And you don't have any other information, right?"

She sighed. "I should probably confess that I phoned

Chuck's sister."

"You did what?" he roared.

"Yeah, I wanted to ask her some questions. And apparently Chuck was at the pub with a friend. I wanted to contact that friend and just see what Chuck's mind-set was like."

"And what difference would his mind-set be?"

"I don't know. Maybe Chuck was afraid that somebody was following him or that he had a recent confrontation with someone. You know how people get that instinct that says somebody's out here. But I obviously can't talk to Chuck in his condition, and his sister was overwhelmed, so I just thought maybe if I could talk to this friend of Chuck's."

"And was it Dante?"

"Yeah, that's the name. And I have his number."

"I'll talk to him," Mack said in a stern voice.

She hesitated, then asked, "Why?"

"Because I know the guy."

"That's probably a good reason *not* to talk to him. You can be a bit of a, you know, a hardheaded bully sometimes."

He snorted at that. "And you just think you can get everything you want with honey."

"It works much better. I'll call him right now." And, with that, she hung up and dialed as fast as she could to make sure that she got in ahead of Mack. When a man answered the other end, she asked to speak with Dante.

"It's my cell phone," he snapped. "So who else do you think would be answering it?"

Doreen winced. "Chuck's sister gave me the number, and she wasn't so sure it was current. I was just trying to make sure it was you."

"How's Chuck?" he asked abruptly.

"Not good." Dante cursed, and she heard the frustration in his voice. "And that's why I'm calling you. I think it might be connected to a case up here in Kelowna."

"What case?" he asked suspiciously. "Are you a cop?"

"Nope, I'm not a cop," she said cheerfully, "but I have a close friend who was shot here recently too."

"Who?"

"Mack. Corporal Mack Moreau."

"What? Big Mack was shot?" he cried out in horror.

"Yeah, he's okay. He's been released from the hospital. I told him that I would call you, and he was irritated at me for getting ahead of him because he wanted to talk to you."

"Of course he did." Dante started to laugh. "But, if you got the jump on Mack, that's too funny. So what is it you want to ask?"

"What was Chuck's state of mind when he left the pub that night before he got shot?"

"He was fine. He'd had a few beers, but he was happy. He didn't seem to be stressed."

"So there was no mention of anything going wrong in his life? No mention about him potentially feeling like he was being followed, nothing like that? No confrontations? Nothing about a case being reopened?"

"No, nothing like that at all. Is that what this is all going back to, that property development scam?"

"I think so," she agreed, "at least that's the only way we know to connect Mack to any of this."

"That's all nonsense too. I mean, Chuck went to Mack. So I mean, I guess it makes sense that they would target Mack, but I don't know why now. It was a long time ago."

"That's what I'm trying to figure out. What on earth would have brought this all back up to the forefront? Did anybody get released from jail? Did anybody bring new charges? Has somebody threatened Chuck? It's those kinds of things that we must find out."

"I don't think anybody threatened Chuck. He was always a happy-go-lucky guy. He was just one of those really good buddies to have around."

She winced, hearing the past tense in his word choice. "And you didn't leave the pub at the same time?"

"I left a few minutes afterward, but I went in the opposite direction."

"Do you happen to know what street corner that pub is on?"

"Yeah, down on Thurlow."

"Oh interesting," she murmured. "Kind of like downtown area."

"Yes, and no. Do you know the area?"

"I've been to Vancouver a fair bit, just not for a while," she said. "So I'm not real familiar with that area."

"It's a seedy part of town, but then that's where we live, so we're used to it."

"The thing is, Lisa told me how Chuck wasn't robbed. His wallet was still on him, with his clothing, his boots. I mean, it's not as if we can pin this down to a robbery or anything like that. Per Lisa, this wasn't a drive-by shooting, The cops think someone on foot approached Chuck and shot him. Nobody else mentioned anything else, except for the fact that they found Chuck shot and bleeding on the street."

"No, and that's concerning too. A robbery I could see, but no need to actually shoot the guy to rob him."

"I wonder," she muttered. "I wonder if there are any street cameras."

"Of course there are street cameras, but I don't know if any are around there." Then his voice rose slightly. "The cops should have already taken a look at that."

"Yep, maybe. Anyway, when Mack calls you, feel free to tell him that I got to you first." She laughed.

She heard the smile in Dante's voice when he said, "Will do. Obviously you two are good friends."

"Yep, we sure are," she muttered. "And believe me. The fact that somebody shot Mack just means that I'm even more determined to track down this gunman."

"You think somebody'll come after him again?"

"If they tried once and failed, they must have had a motive for starting this process. What are the chances that they're willing to walk away now?"

"If it were me, I wouldn't," Dante confirmed, "but I wouldn't fail in the first place."

She winced at that. "Got it. Please call me, if you come up with any idea of what's going on or anybody else I can talk to who might have seen Chuck on the way home or who Chuck may have been talking to on the phone recently—anything like that. Oh, by the way, Chuck's phone was missing. I presume he had it on him in the pub?"

"Yes," Dante said, a resigned tone to his voice. "And that, of course, would have been something quite helpful to the shooter, I presume."

"Yep, sure would have been because, if there were any text messages, phone threats, anything like that, it would have been on his phone. So it makes sense that his phone was taken."

"I don't know who would have done this, but, if you can tie it back to those developer scammers, do so. They hurt a lot of people."

"And were you affected personally?"

"I worked in the industry along with Chuck. So I lost that job, but I got another one pretty soon afterward. However, I didn't have any money to own a home. Usually the middle-aged or older generations can afford these things, and the younger generation is in the process of saving for them, hoping that, when they get older, they can get something themselves."

"That's logical," she muttered. Her mind was grasping for something, anything to jump to. "What about Celia? Did you ever have anything to do with her?"

"Celia Farleigh? No." He snorted. "She's a cow."

At that, Doreen winced, having heard that phrase a time or two directed at her. "So she was like ugly?"

"No, I wouldn't say she was so much ugly. I mean, the outside appearance was pretty decent, but the inside packaging was lacking. People like that are those you always have to watch out for."

"She seems to be pretty determined that her Vaughn was innocent."

"*Her Vaughn?* Old man Bowman?"

"Or her Rodney was innocent."

"What do you mean, her Rodney?"

"Oh, don't you know? Celia married Rodney Bowman twelve, thirteen years or so ago."

First came a shocked gasp, and then he roared, "Get out of town."

Not exactly sure how that phrase ever made sense to anybody, Doreen murmured, "It's true."

"Well, if that doesn't beat all. And that just makes Rodney even guiltier in my eyes."

"Why is that?"

"Celia was really close with old man Vaughn, and he had money and used it to spoil her rotten. I don't know whether any kind of other relationship was going on there or not, but she was milking him for all he was worth. I think back then the old man was dating her mother, so it was cozy for both mother and daughter to be gifted so much money. When he went to jail, that money dried up."

"I don't know how much that money dried up though, considering she ended up marrying the grandson."

"Exactly, so how much of this was just a big con on her part?"

"Do you think she was involved in the property development scam?"

"I don't think so." He pondered that for a moment. "As much as I'd like to say yes, I don't think so. She wasn't old enough, mature enough, to get into those kinds of dealings, so I don't think that that's possible. But Terrence, the father—between Vaughn, the old guy, and Rodney, Vaughn's grandson—the father was the one was most likely to have been involved, wasn't he? Of course he died way back when. Now he was involved, but he skated on the charges. And the old man passed away in prison."

Interesting how everyone kept track of the old man. Then the case had been big news back then.

"Yeah, the old man didn't make it out of jail. Yet he kept saying he was innocent right up to the end, as far as I know," he said, "Yet we all knew he wasn't innocent."

"When you say, you all knew, is that true?" she asked curiously. "Like, I mean, did you really know back then, or did you just assume that Vaughn was a part of this? Or did you come to know for sure later? What if it was actually the son, Terrence, but the grandfather Vaughn went to jail to protect him?"

And here again was another moment of silence, as Dante thought about that. "In that case then Vaughn was a fool. Because that boy of his, Terrence, was just as bad. I don't know about Rodney. I haven't had anything to do with any of them in a very long time."

"But now that Chuck's been shot, if you had anything to do with that case," she warned Dante, "I'd watch your back."

"Yeah, you're not kidding," he growled, disgruntled. "And who needs that at this stage of our life?"

"That's why I'm wondering how much any of this comes back to the people who may be still alive now from that scam of fifteen years ago. Whether Rodney or his father. What about Terrence?"

"He's long dead."

"Interesting," she murmured. "Yeah, just so many people are involved that you wonder who was hiding the facts back then … and who was protecting whom. Although Terrence and Vaughn are both gone, we still have Lenny missing and Rodney here in town. Mack got shot. Chuck, as the whistle-blower, was shot a day earlier and is seriously injured, so whoever is behind this can't come from too wide of a suspect pool."

"I don't know why anybody would protect any of that lot. They had no problem stealing from old people, young people. As long as they got the money, they couldn't have cared less where it came from or who suffered from their actions. They were all about selfish greed."

They ended the call, and Doreen considered how Dante had said all the right things. And how Mack and Dante go way back.

So why did Doreen feel like Dante had lied to her?

Chapter 23

AFTER THAT CONVERSATION Doreen took the animals down to the river at the back of her yard. If nothing else, she needed a chance to clear her head and to sort things out. She also wouldn't mind talking to Roger again, who had walked up to talk to her about what he knew initially. With that thought in mind, she turned to go in the direction of Rosemoor. The animals happily rambled along, as she headed toward Nan.

Doreen answered her phone, as Nan called her. "Hey, I'm just walking your way."

"Perfect," Nan said cheerfully. "I was hoping to convince you to come down and to have a cup of tea."

"Are you okay?" she asked.

"I'm fine," she replied, "just a little sad. We lost somebody last night."

"Oh, Nan, I'm so sorry," Doreen cried out softly.

"It happens. It is life here in an old folks' home," Nan said. "We're just all waiting our turn."

Doreen winced at that reminder. "And yet most of the time it doesn't make you quite this depressed."

"She was a nice lady. I mean, she wasn't necessarily *my*

kind of nice lady, but a death always reminds you that we're mortal and that our time is rapidly coming toward us."

"It's coming for all of us," Doreen murmured gently.

"I know, but, in your case, chances are it'll be a lot longer away."

"I hope so, for you and for me." Doreen laughed. "I'd really like a chance to live before that happens."

"Exactly, that's why I keep telling you that you need to move on Mack."

"I don't know about moving on Mack," she replied cautiously, "but at least appreciating the time and relationships I do have."

"That's a start."

"I'm halfway to your place right now. I was hoping to talk to that older man who came to see me with the information about the property development scam," she explained.

"Oh, Roger is here too," Nan noted. "I'll let him know you're coming."

"Good enough."

As soon as Doreen got around to the corner of the Rosemoor property, she stopped and stared at the rosebush, immediately saddened by the memory of Mack being shot and falling here. Mugs walked closer and sniffed the bush several times, then looked back at her and woofed. Doreen walked over to where the car had been parked, then turned and faced where she and Mack had been walking that fateful night. No way that the shooter wouldn't have seen them approach.

As Doreen looked around, it didn't matter whether she drove or walked via the creek or the main roads, or whether she entered through the front door or Nan's patio, she would pass by this very spot.

At that thought, Doreen remembered what Laura had said about how the gunman would go in and see somebody. So who the devil would he see? Or was that just a cover story to throw everybody off? Doreen was missing vital pieces of information yet.

As she studied Rosemoor, she realized that someone had knowingly said something about Doreen and Mack attending that night. Although … she frowned, then sighed. It had been a celebration of sorts for Doreen. So anyone in town could have found out about it.

Anyway Doreen decided to run it by Nan anyway.

As soon as she and her animals had walked onto Nan's patio, exchanging their usual happy greetings and treats, Doreen sat down across from her grandmother and whispered, with a gleam in her eye, "I have something for you to focus on."

Nan raised her eyebrows. "Have you got something for me to sleuth?"

"Somewhat, but we have to be very cautious about it."

At that, Nan slowly nodded. "What's up?"

And she told her about her theory about somebody in this home having told the gunman about how Doreen and Mack were coming down to the party.

She stared at her in shock. "Oh, I don't like the sound of that."

"Nope, I don't either." As she explained her theory a little further, Nan just stared at her and shook her head.

"But who would do that?" she cried out in a horrified whisper.

"The question is, was it done innocently?" Doreen narrowed her gaze. "Or was it done with the intent to hurt

Mack?"

"Or you," Nan straightened up and stared at her with that gimlet eye. "We cannot lose sight of the fact that this could very well be connected to you or your cold cases."

Doreen slowly nodded. "I know, but it's unlikely at this stage. I'm pretty sure it's related to Mack and one of his prior cases."

Nan tapped the table. "I need to bring in some help to do this."

"I don't even know who we would ask." And Doreen stopped, lowered her voice, and added, "We can't have too many people in the know."

"No, you're right there. The wrong person will just cause us more trouble."

"And, once you let the cat out of the bag, the chance of us ever putting a stop to this is pretty slim."

"No, I agree."

At that, they heard the *thud* of a cane on the door frame in Nan's apartment. Nan hopped up and walked inside. When she returned, Richie hobbled behind her. She pointed at the empty patio chair. "Sit." Richie sat.

Doreen had to smile at the immediacy of his actions. She looked at him and grinned. "She's got you well trained."

He rolled his eyes at her. "I was married for forty-five years. Your grandmother is just following along with a great tradition." Mugs walked closer to Richie and got a welcomed behind-the-ear scrubbing. Happy with that, Mugs plunked to the patio floor at Doreen's feet.

She laughed and reached down to pet Mugs. Then she turned to face Richie. "I don't know whether Nan asked you to come or not, but we've got a problem." The smile fell off his face as Doreen explained.

He whistled. "Now that is not good news. At the same time, you're right, it makes a whole lot more sense. The gunman had to know that Mack was coming."

"Or Doreen," Nan interjected quickly.

Richie stopped to consider that and then nodded. "Again quite true. He had to know that you were both coming, regardless of who it was he was gunning for. The fact that he shot Mack leads me to think that it was Mack he was after, but we can't be too sure about that."

"No, we can't," Nan agreed. "And I'm not willing to put my granddaughter's life in jeopardy on a hunch."

"Ooh no, definitely not. We need a whole lot more to go on than that." Richie looked over at Nan. "We did ask a lot of people here to come to Doreen's celebratory event," he admitted. "It never occurred to us that we were potentially talking to the suspect involved in an attempted murderer— or his inside man."

"And I don't think we necessarily did," Doreen pointed out. "I think we invited somebody who either gave out that information innocently or for a reason that we have yet to uncover. Do I still think this is all connected to the same problem from fifteen years ago? Yes," she added, with a nod.

"I don't see how it can't be, considering what we know to date," Richie stated, sharing a nod with Nan.

Her grandmother added, "But that doesn't mean somebody didn't add another layer to it." Nan stared at Doreen.

At that, Doreen asked her, "Are you trying to pull this around to somebody wanted to get rid of me again?"

"It would have been a pretty easy way to do it."

"But they didn't though," Doreen pointed out. "And, if that's what they were trying to do, they failed in a big way."

"And that just makes me wonder too," Richie said. "I

mean, what kind of a gunman would make a mistake like that?"

"A nervous one. Potentially one who's never shot anybody before," Nan suggested.

"Maybe, based on what we know of this old case of Mack's, where they were conning people, not shooting them," Doreen argued. "Still, what would be the driving need to shoot Mack now? Because that's what I don't get. Everything in the case was investigated like fifteen years ago."

At that, both Nan and Richie nodded.

Doreen continued. "That's what I'm trying to figure out. Something must have happened. There must have been a trigger to bring this old business to a head right now. Not just Mack's shooting, but somebody shot Chuck a day earlier." And she explained about Chuck down on the Vancouver coast.

"Oh, wow," Richie replied. "Surely that indicates that this is related to Mack's case and not one of yours, right?"

"Exactly." Doreen considered that. "And I guess you didn't hold back from passing around invitations for the Rosemoor party, including who and what was going on, did you?"

Richie and Nan both faced Doreen and slowly shook their heads. Nan got a worried look on her face.

Doreen repeated, "Still it could have been anybody, from staff to residents to family and friends. It could have been just an innocent word dropped at the wrong time."

"Or at the right time," Richie added in a low tone. "We can't forget the fact that the end result was very directed. And Mack suffered for that."

Doreen nodded. "And also the fact that this shooter missed. Whether he was after me or trying to kill Mack, I still believe that nobody comes with a gun to wound somebody. They come to kill."

At that, both of them looked at her and slowly nodded.

"So, does anybody here have something against Mack? Something that they would aid and abet somebody else to fulfilling their own revenge mess?"

They both looked at her in horror.

"I would hope not," Richie shuddered. "That would not be good."

"Maybe not be good," Doreen admitted, "but we know that it happens, and it happens a little too often."

They both sat, either shocked or considering this further.

Doreen picked up the teapot and filled their cups. In a low voice, she asked, "What about Laura?"

They both lifted their heads and stared at her in shock.

"Why would you say anything about Laura?" Nan asked.

"Because she saw the shooter."

"Sure, but that doesn't mean that she saw him ahead of time or that she said anything else to him. And she's the one who said that he was waiting for somebody inside."

Doreen nodded at that. "I know. I know. And what about Roger, who walked to my house to give me information on the property development scam?"

At that, Richie snorted. "He's got one, two, maybe three weeks left of life. I can't imagine anybody that close to death wanting to take revenge right before going to their grave."

"Is Roger that close to dying?" Doreen asked, staring at Richie.

He nodded. "Quite likely."

"Does Laura have a boyfriend?" Doreen asked him.

He shook his head. "I don't think so."

At that, Nan snorted. "She's the one who is sweet on

Mack. She'd never do anything to hurt him."

Doreen hesitated before finally blurting out, "Would she do anything to hurt me?"

Nan stared at her, her mouth turning into a rosebud shape. "Oh my. I have no idea.'

"Somebody who might want Mack might shoot me to free him up. But then it goes against all the suppositions," Doreen corrected, "that we have gathered so far. Although the shooter fired a second shot in my direction."

"And it is only supposition that he was aiming at you," Richie reminded them both.

"Exactly. Which isn't a great way to do an investigation. But, so far, we're running thin on facts and even thinner on evidence. And that's pretty upsetting." Doreen stood. "I'll head over to Mack's to see if I can jog his memory. And to hear what he found out after talking to a friend of his."

Mugs got up and walked over to say goodbye to Nan, then nudged a sleeping Goliath, curled up on his usual flower box in the sun.

"The bottom line is somebody knew, somehow the shooter knew that Mack would be coming down that pathway or at least heading to Rosemoor for that celebration. The shooter, parked where he was, would have seen anybody coming and going. So it could have been that he knew we were coming down the pathway or just that we would be attending, and he was waiting here to have us show up."

They both sat there and contemplated everybody in the home.

"Hundreds of people are here," Nan said helplessly. "And we don't know who all they know in town."

"I know. Which is why I was trying to figure out if there was a way to narrow down the possibilities. But it sounds like there isn't. Plus I'm not sure this inside-man hypothesis works." Doreen smiled gently. "Anyway, I'll go talk to Mack. He'll just tell me that I'm thinking too hard. I'll talk to you two later."

At that, Nan nodded slowly. "You be careful, please."

"I will. Although I still think this is about Mack, not me."

"Yet we can't be sure," Richie pointed out. "And it'll break your grandmother's heart if anything happens to you."

Doreen leaned over, gave her grandmother a hug, and kissed her gently on the cheek. "I promise I'll be fine."

And, with that, she quickly picked up Thaddeus, parked him on her shoulder, and said, "Come on, Goliath, Mugs. We have some sleuthing to do."

"Do you know where Mack lives?" Richie asked.

She stopped and frowned. "You know something? I need to call him and get that address."

"I have it," Nan said. She wrote it down on a piece of paper.

"And how did you get it?"

"I've known where he lived for a long time. You never want to be without a cop friend. They're very handy to have around."

Doreen chuckled. "Isn't that the truth." And, with that, she quickly escaped.

Standing outside, she looked at the address and nodded. "We'll drive to that one."

Chapter 24

A S SHE WALKED up to her house from the river, Doreen pondered her open kitchen door. It was banging back and forth in the wind. She looked down at Mugs. "Did we lock it? Rather I guess it no longer locks and we need to fix that. And obviously we forgot to set the alarm again. I won't tell Mack if you don't."

He stared at the door, just like she did. Slowly she walked into the kitchen. She heard sounds inside, and immediately Mugs broke into action and raced into the house, tugging the leash free from her hands. Chaos ensued, as his barking overshadowed someone's shrieks. Doreen raced to the front door, assuming the other guy would escape.

But instead she found a woman, standing on the seat of one of her two chairs there, screaming, "Get away from me. Get away from me."

Doreen reached down and hauled Mugs back from the woman, but he wasn't willing to calm down. "Who are you?" Doreen asked in astonishment. "What are you doing in my house?"

"I'm Laura." The woman looked at her and pointed at

the dog. "Get that thing away from me."

"*That thing*," Doreen snapped, "lives here."

"And what about that thing?" Laura now pointed to Goliath, who was slinking toward Laura and coming up from the side, as if to attack. Immediately Laura shrieked, jumped down, and ran across the room.

It was all Doreen could do to hold Mugs back. Something about a person who was afraid of animals just made the animals crowd them even more. "You want to stop screaming? It's upsetting the animals."

Laura finally slowed to sobbing, then to gasps, followed by hiccoughs. "My God." She shuddered. "How can you stand to be around them?"

"They are part of my family, so that's not an issue. Now what are you doing in my house?"

The woman looked at her, looked at the front door, then the still-open kitchen door, and said, "The door was unlocked."

Immediately Doreen frowned at her. "What do you mean, it was unlocked? And, even if it were, you don't just walk into somebody else's house."

"I called out to see if you were here," Laura stated in a reasonable tone. "When you didn't answer, I opened the door and called again, thinking that maybe you were upstairs."

It was almost feasible, but something was off about the woman. "And then what?" Doreen asked, trying to keep her suspicions in check. "You just decided to sit in my home and wait?"

"I wanted to talk to you. And I didn't want to go to work too early because then I would just have been put to work that much earlier. So it just seemed to make sense to sit here and wait."

"You don't just walk into somebody's house uninvited," Doreen repeated, staring at the woman, wondering if she was quite all there. "Not even to wait for them to show up. You come back at another time, or you phone ahead, or you sit outside and wait."

At that, Laura's head came up and sniffed. "You don't have to be mean about it."

Doreen reached for her patience, but, even now, Mugs was trying to get closer to her, as in protecting her from this crazy woman. "I am protecting myself *and* all my animals from unwanted strangers in my home," she muttered.

"I don't understand the animal part at all." Laura inched toward the front door. "Have you got a good hold on them?"

"I do."

"Good." And she bolted for the front door.

Immediately Mugs lunged again, but Doreen managed to hold him back.

Laura froze.

"I don't know what about you is bothering him," Doreen noted, "but he's not happy."

"I can see that," Laura snapped. "Those animals are dangerous. You should have them put down."

At that, Doreen narrowed her gaze. "I *really* wouldn't say that to anyone with pets again," she said, with exaggerated gentleness. "These animals never hurt anybody."

"Oh, that's not what I've heard." Laura glared at Mugs. "Rumors have it that they're very dangerous and that they've bitten all kinds of people."

"If they have, it's because those other people were hurting me."

At that, the woman looked at her. And then she

shrugged. "I doubt it. Anybody can see they're dangerous."

"Before I call the cops, can we go back to the beginning here? Why did you come to see me?"

At that, Laura's head went back up again, as if she were afraid of being criticized once more.

Doreen took a deep breath, trying to control her temper. The nerve of this woman ...

"Because I heard you talking to your grandmother. And my name came up."

At that, Doreen stared at Laura. "You *heard* me talking to her?"

"Yes, and I didn't have anything to do with the attack on Mack."

"I'm glad to hear that, but I don't think you *heard* me talking to her."

"Yes, I did. I often sit outside of Nan's apartment and visit."

"And yet you couldn't have been sitting there and visiting if you *heard* that conversation."

"Why not?" she asked in surprise.

"Because, while I was sitting there visiting Nan, nobody else was around."

"You didn't look around the corner," Laura said in a weirdly superior tone of voice. "And voices do carry. You hear all kinds of things."

"And is that what you do? Spy on all the residents, while you're sitting there on your breaks?" she asked. "I can't imagine they'd appreciate that."

"I'm sure they don't know." Laura shrugged. "And most of them are so old anyway, I don't think they really understand what's going on half the time. Really, some of those people need to be taken into hand. I'm sure a place with more care would be better for a lot of them. You can't just have them running around town, doing their own thing."

"Why not?" Doreen asked in a dry tone. "I mean, after all, they are all adults."

"No, you don't understand. Some of them are like …" And she lifted a hand and circled her ear.

"Meaning that their dementia or Alzheimer's is kicking in?"

"Or just plain crazy. Did you know they have sex?" she cried out in a horrified whisper.

Doreen pinched the bridge of her nose, shaking her head. "You do know that a lot of people in this world have sex?"

"Yes, but these people are"—and she lowered her voice again and looked around, as if afraid she would be over-heard—"they're old. Like *old*-old."

At that, Doreen chuckled. "I did some research on that for a cold case once, and the prevalence of STDs in these retirement homes is worse than it is for the general population."

At that, Laura gasped and clapped a hand over her mouth. "That's just disgusting."

Doreen wasn't even sure just what to say to that. "Why? Because they're older?"

"No, not older. *Old*."

"If you say so, but I don't think age makes much difference."

"Sure it does. I mean, who wants to have sex with somebody who's old and gray, with saggy skin and wrinkles everywhere?"

"Maybe another person who is old and gray, with saggy wrinkles everywhere," Doreen snapped back. "Sex doesn't have to be about bodies. It's supposed to be about more than that."

"That's only true if it's supposed to be *more than* bodies. But, for a lot of people, it's just about bodies."

"Then, if it's just bodies and each of the bodies is happy, what difference does it make, and what has it got to do with you?"

Laura leaned against the front door, her fingers flicking nervously. "Do you think Mack's old?"

At that, Doreen snorted. "No, he's a male in his prime. Do you think you're old?"

Laura's eyes widened. "I'm not that old. Certainly not too old for Mack."

"Is that what this is about? Are you trying to get close to Mack?" Doreen asked gently.

The woman shrugged, but a light filled her gaze. "I mean, he's a nice man," Laura explained. "Anybody would be happy to get close to him."

Doreen bit her lip. "And what if he already has a relationship?" she asked curiously.

"Who though? Every time I've seen him, he's alone." And then she snorted. "I mean, if it would be with anybody, it'd probably be you, but I can't see that either. Especially not with these vicious animals." She glared at Goliath, who chose that moment to shoot a rear leg sky-high and clean his butt.

As the insults were so blatant, it was hard for Doreen to continue to be nice to this woman. "First of all, Mack loves animals. He loves my animals. Second, you find it hard to believe that Mack would like me?" And then she sighed. "Look. Why are you really here?"

"It occurred to me that maybe Mack does like you, so,

you know, maybe if he does, and I spent some time with you, he would like me."

"You know that's not how it works, right?"

"Well, it could. He would like me if he just had a chance to get to know me. And he can't get to know me because he never spends any time around me. We're not in the same circles, so how else am I supposed to get him to see me?"

Doreen shook her head. Laura's "logic" was a little convoluted. Yet Nan said everybody liked Laura. Doreen had trouble reconciling that comment with the odd woman who broke into her home and who then constantly berated Doreen and her animals. "You know that Mack's super-busy, right? I mean, he's always working on cases. He's kind of a workaholic."

"Oh, I can fix that," she said confidently.

"He's also …" Doreen hesitated, "he's quite a bit younger than you are."

The woman looked at her. "Do you think I'm too old for him?"

"I think, if he cared for the soul of a person, their age or their old wrinkly bodies wouldn't matter to him. I'm just not sure that he cares for people who hate animals. Plus there is quite an age gap for him to consider with you."

Laura frowned at that.

Doreen suggested, "Aren't there some men closer to your age, potentially ones who maybe work at Rosemoor?" She wanted to say those who *live at Rosemoor* but knew that would get her in trouble.

"I keep looking for somebody there," Laura admitted, "but it's a really lonely world, and it's hard to meet people."

"I agree." Doreen really did understand. "I do know, however, that Mack has a lot of people in his life already."

At that, Laura's shoulders slumped. "You're trying to tell me nicely that there's no room for me, aren't you?"

"I'm telling you that you might do better if you went looking for somebody else."

Laura paused, pouted. "But I really like Mack. I like big men, like Mack."

"Why don't you join a walking club or a cooking club or take dance lessons or something, where you would enjoy meeting men."

Laura frowned at that. "What if they say they don't want anything to do with me?"

"Then you move on," Doreen said gently. "And you try again. Maybe take art classes or join a bridge club or something."

Laura pondered it. "Maybe. I guess I need to look at someone else." And then she turned to focus on Doreen. "I mean, I guess if he likes you, he's really not the kind of person who would like me."

"There's nothing wrong with you," Doreen said, trying to help a lost soul here.

The woman looked at her and smiled. "I know," she declared. "I'm a gift. But, if Mack likes you, he obviously wouldn't appreciate me."

And, with that, she walked out the front door, leaving a very stunned Doreen behind.

Chapter 25

DOREEN STILL REELED from the verbal blows that she'd just been handed by Laura, yet chuckled inside at the total absurdity of it all. Now Doreen wondered how to even explain any of this to Mack, wondering if she should even try. Still, Doreen intended to go to Mack's house as planned, so she packed up the animals, who moved excitedly around her feet. It took a bit to get them in her vehicle because they were so hyper from their interactions with the crazy screaming interloper. "Come on. Let's go see Mack."

Ever since she mentioned Mack's name, Mugs wouldn't stop woofing, and even Goliath was howling at her.

"Okay, okay, but we have to get there first."

Finally she got them into the car and backed out of the garage. With the address in her head, she slowly drove toward his place. She parked outside the residence and exited her car to study the dark brick bungalow. "It's not what I expected," she announced and then winced. "Yet I'm not sure what I did expect." Of course she much preferred her place, but then Mack hadn't been given a house by his grandmother. Doreen sighed at that.

"Nan, you have no idea how grateful I am that you are

you. Every day, in so many ways, I keep getting reminded of how blessed I am."

She walked up to the front door and rang the doorbell. Almost immediately the door was opened by Nick. He grinned. "This is a pleasant surprise."

"Yeah, says you. Wait until I tell you why I'm here."

Nick opened his mouth to ask, but Mugs, already sensing who was inside, tore the leash from Doreen's fingers, and raced in to see Mack. She sighed. "I hope that means we're allowed in," she asked, "because we'll have a heck of a time trying to separate Mugs and Mack."

Nick laughed. "You're more than welcome to come in. It'll help him with his bad mood."

"Why is he in a bad mood?"

"Because the police won't let him into the investigation," he noted in a low tone.

She raised an eyebrow, walked into the living room, and saw Mack sitting in a big easy chair, with Mugs in his lap, cleaning his face.

She chuckled. "You wouldn't come to us," she said, "so we came to you."

He looked over at her, and she saw the warm welcome in his gaze.

"And, of course, I can commiserate because I have absolutely experienced going through what you're going through."

"And what exactly is that?" he asked curiously.

"Being kept out of investigations by the police," she stated gleefully.

He glared at her. "I *am* the police."

"You're *one* of the police. This just goes to show you what it'd be like if you ever retired."

He shook his head. "I'm not retiring," he announced. "I have lots of work left to do."

"Yep, I know that feeling too. Too bad people won't let me get at it." And then she stared at him pointedly.

He groaned. "Did you have any other reason to come by, other than to bug me?"

"I did have some information, and then I had a break-in, and then I had to *entertain* a lovesick suitor of yours, and I just, you know, have so much going on," she explained. "I wasn't sure what I was supposed to do with any of it. So I came here."

He stopped and stared at her in shock. Nick walked around to stand at Mack's side to stare at her in shock also.

She shrugged. "What can I say? You're a popular guy."

Mack looked at his brother, back at her, and asked Nick, "Do you have *any* idea what she's talking about?"

Nick shook his head, sat down across from him on the couch. "But then I rarely understand what she's trying to say."

She fisted her hands on her hips and glared at Nick.

He chuckled. "That look? You really should patent it."

"If I knew how," she said immediately, "I would. There's money in patents."

Nick sighed. "But you're fine for money for this year, aren't you?"

"Yep, I got my ten thousand dollar reward check from Bernard deposited in the bank," she said smugly.

"You should be okay, but you probably want to make sure," Mack shared in a silky tone, "that it cleared the bank."

She glared at him. "You're just trying to upset me."

"Now why would I do that?" He laughed. "I am really happy to see you."

"Good." Doreen sighed heavily. She glanced over at Nick, whose grin almost reached his ears as his gaze went from Doreen to Mack and back. "Your brother thinks we make a great couple." She plopped down on the couch beside Nick.

Thaddeus popped out from under her hair and screamed, "Mack, Mack," and flew across the short span to land on top of Mugs. Mugs immediately turned, snapping at him. Undeterred, Thaddeus walked up Mugs's back, up his neck, atop Mugs's head, and then stepped cheerfully over to Mack and rubbed his feathered head against Mack's cheek.

Mack reached up, closed his eyes, smiled, and just cuddled the bird.

"See? You didn't realize you needed us. We put a smile on your face. Okay, so a lot of time you get angry with us, but, if you take the good with the bad, generally we're a good deal."

He looked over at her, his lips twitching. "Generally, yes, but there are times …"

"There are times," she nodded agreeably, "when you completely ruin everything in my world." His jaw dropped. She burst out laughing.

Mack sighed and looked over at his brother. "See? See how she is?"

"Yep, I see entirely." Nick's face lit up with a huge smile. "And I'm thoroughly jealous."

"Jealous of what?" Doreen asked, looking at him curiously.

"Your relationship. You two really understand each other, and, although you're still dancing around that whole relationship stuff, it's obvious that you're very well matched. You get each other. You respect each other, and, even when you're not getting your own way, you're both being very good about it."

She looked over at Mack and shrugged. "Do you know what he's talking about?"

Mack grinned. "Oh, yeah. I know what he's talking about, and so do you. You just won't admit it."

She smiled, turned, and looked at Nick, and, with a sudden insight, added, "Okay. Do either of you know of anyone interested in meeting a slightly off sixty-year-old woman who hates animals but loves big men, like your size?"

Nick narrowed his gaze and shook his head. "Very odd conversation, Doreen. And, just for the record, never set me up. *Ever.*"

She looked over at Mack, who stared at her, obviously confused.

"What are you talking about?" Mack asked.

"Laura."

"Laura? Laura who?"

"The one who works at Rosemoor. Remember? She's the one who spoke to the shooter outside Rosemoor."

"Right." Mack nodded. "When did you talk to her?"

"I returned from Rosemoor earlier, and she was inside my house."

His smile immediately dropped from his face, and he narrowed his gaze at her. "What do you mean, she was *inside* your house?"

"You heard me," she said cautiously. "She was *inside* my house."

"Good Lord." Nick straightened. "Why?"

"She was looking for me apparently, and, when she didn't find me, she decided to make herself at home."

Mack reached up his one free hand to rub his temples.

"Was she … okay?"

"She was probably as okay as she can be, but I guess it will take a little bit to explain," she said, "so I'll start at the beginning."

By the time she was done, including Laura's trick for memorizing the license plate letters and Laura's thoughts about anybody at Rosemoor having sex, Mack's jaw headed to the floor, and Nick was mute.

Doreen waited for one of the brothers to speak up. "So, what should we do about Laura?"

Mack spoke first. "This puts the veracity of her statement about the shooter into serious jeopardy. I'll contact the captain."

Nick nodded. "I'm no doctor, but I feel like she needs psychiatric help and could be a danger to the residents at Rosemoor. I would recommend that she be fired. I'll make a suggestion to the overseer."

Doreen grimaced. "I'm not trying to discredit her or to get her fired. Honestly I think she's mostly lonely—and odd, yes."

Mack and Nick shared a glance, and Doreen wanted to know what that wordless look meant. Then the two brothers nodded at some agreement.

Nick began. "You are very kind-hearted to find the good in Laura, but I would feel much better if the residents at Rosemoor, like your grandmother, were protected from Laura. It seems she hates animals and old people."

Doreen frowned. "And she's listening in on their private conversations too." She nodded. "Nan and the others must be protected."

Mack nodded. "I agree. Doreen, you *do* understand what goes on at the old folks' homes, right?"

"Are you kidding?" She wrinkled up her nose. "Whether I want to or not, I still have Nan as my grandmother, who's an open and free-loving spirit," she said, with an eye roll. "I'd just as soon not hear the sexual details though."

Mack's grin flashed. "I knew I liked your nan."

She sighed. "Everybody likes my nan," she muttered. She looked over at Nick. "Have you ever met her?"

He shook his head. "No, but that's definitely on my list."

"She's a sweetheart. And I was thinking as I came up to your house, how much I owe her for giving her house to me. I don't know where I'd be without her." And, even at that admission, her voice choked up. "So, as crazy as Laura may be, do we think she's involved in shooting Mack?"

Mack frowned. "Casting aside her alleged gun proficiency, why would this woman who claims to like me then shoot me?"

Nick nodded. "Yeah, what would be her motive?"

Doreen counted off as she offered two suggestions. "One, she could have a childlike mentality and think that punching a guy in the belly on the kindergarten playground is her way of showing she cares. Two, remember that old saying about, if she can't have you, then no one can?"

Nick shrugged and looked at his brother. "Both valid."

Mack shook his head. "Not relevant with all the facts. Look at Chuck. He was shot. Not by some crazy woman either." Mack sighed. "Doreen, you *must* set your security alarm every time you leave the house. That crazy woman should never have gained access inside your house," he declared. "Except for that not small issue of a broken door."

"No, she shouldn't have," she winced, "I have to admit how that made me pause for a moment."

"I'm really glad to hear that it made you pause, but that also means that you left without putting on your security," Mack snapped, clearly warming up to one of his biggest lectures.

She held out a hand. "If I'm not allowed to lecture you about getting shot, you're not allowed to lecture me about not setting the security every time."

"You can't lecture me about getting shot," he snapped in disgust. "I'd never lecture *you* about getting shot."

She crossed her legs and also her arms. "Really? I'm pretty sure you've lectured me about getting hurt every time."

He frowned. "I didn't know I would get shot."

She raised an eyebrow. "Like I knew any of the other times before I got hurt?"

"You were putting your nose into places where it didn't belong."

"And, until we get to the bottom of this shooter case, we have no idea what kind of mess you've gotten yourself into," she said pointedly. And, with that said, she deliberately turned to Nick. "Has he been behaving himself?"

Mack's brother burst out into rich laughter that filled the room. "You know something? He's been pining for you," he said gently. "So I'm really glad you came by."

She beamed. "That's a lovely thing to say. And thanks for listening to my weird theories." She looked back at Mack. "Did you solve it yet?"

"No, I didn't solve it yet." Then he straightened and looked at her. "So what'd you find out?"

She gave him an innocent look.

"Oh no, no, no, no, no." He shook his head, then pointed a finger at her. "Give, give, give."

"I'm not sure there's anything to give," she said sadly.

"Did you guys phone Dante?"

Mack nodded. "He didn't seem to have anything to offer."

"Yeah, I wondered about that. Any chance we can get a look at the security cameras on the streets near that pub?"

"Why?"

"Because Chuck was shot on the street, heading out on Thurlow. That's still a pretty major street in Vancouver, yet probably not a whole lot of activity at that commercial downtown location once the bars close, but why can't we get access to the cameras and see whether your friend Dante followed Chuck or not?"

At that, Nick looked at her and then at Mack.

"Are you thinking Dante shot Chuck?" Mack protested immediately. "I've known Dante for years."

"I'm not saying Dante shot Chuck. I'm testing a theory. Yes, you've also known Chuck and Dante for years. And what I have learned over the last few months of working on these cold cases is that we never really know anybody."

Mack nodded and sighed heavily. "Plus once these guys spend time in jail—even Chuck and Dante—they just meet up with more and more criminals, learning more ways to con people."

Just then Mugs jumped off Mack's lap and barked once at the front door and looked back at her.

She hopped to her feet, grabbed his leash, looked at Mack, and asked, "You okay if I take him out into your backyard?"

He nodded immediately.

"I'll take Goliath too. Thaddeus will probably want to stay with you."

But, at that, Thaddeus cried, "Thaddeus is here. Thaddeus is here." He looked at her and flapped his wings. She instinctively held out her arm, and he hopped up on her wrist and walked up to her shoulder. With all the animals in tow, she walked into the kitchen, pulled open the back door, and stepped outside onto a big deck. "Wow." She smiled. "Now this makes sense. This deck redeems the entire house."

She walked down the deck, and, with the animals free to roam, Mugs immediately sniffed out a spot, lifted a leg, and thereafter kept wandering around. She pulled doggie bags from her back pocket and waited for him to do his business. As soon as he was done, she cleaned it up and walked to the back gate beside the garage and peered over the top of the gate into an alleyway. Sure enough, garbage cans were there. She opened the latch, pulled Mugs through, and dropped the bag into the garbage. And then noticed Goliath walking in the opposite direction.

"Goliath, come back here." His ears twitched, as if he were listening but still ignored her. "Don't you do that," she cried out. "All kinds of cars are out there."

His tail twitched at that, giving several sharp flicks in her direction.

"*Great*," she muttered.

Mugs tore his leash away from Doreen's grip and immediately raced after Goliath. And she started after them both, calling out, "That's enough. Get back here."

When they got to the corner, they both stopped, turned, and looked at her, and Mugs immediately dropped his butt onto the ground, as if to say, *Hurry up.* When she caught up with them, she grabbed Mugs's leash once more, and she stared at them. "What's the matter, guys? Why are you out here?"

When she looked up, right around the corner was

parked an empty silver Camry with a dented-in side. She walked around the vehicle and looked at it several times, took a photo of it and its license plate—with an *L* and an *M* in it—and sent it to Mack. She didn't know if it was the vehicle Mack's shooter had used, but it was a little bit too much of a coincidence for her liking.

As she stepped out to head back down Mack's alleyway, she watched as somebody came toward her at a fast clip, his head down, looking at his phone. He wore a baseball cap and sunglasses, was about five-eight. Was it the Camry driver? If so, ... that made him Mack's shooter. She gripped her hand tightly around Mugs's leash and whispered, "This is the guy who shot Mack."

She studied her odds, wondering what her choices were, and then finally, just as he almost reached her, she picked up speed and raced right toward him. At the last minute he looked up, as if to finally take note of her. She hit him square on the nose with her fist and sent him down to the gravel of the alleyway.

The man got up and roared at her, "Hey, what are you doing?"

But she wasn't having any of it. She came up with her fist clenched and plowed into him with another one, right in the jaw.

He stumbled backward and called out, "You're crazy. What are you doing? I don't even know you."

"No," she cried out, "but you will." And she jumped him again.

With him trying to defend himself and also screaming for help, she hit him again and again. And finally big arms wrapped around her, and she was picked up and held off the ground. Screaming, she called out, "Somebody call the police, call the police."

"I am the police," Mack said in disgust.

She twisted and looked at him. "What are you doing picking me up?" she cried out. "Put me down right now," she snapped. "You'll hurt your shoulder."

He sighed and put her down, and she noted Nick was helping the other man to his feet.

"Oh, yeah," she growled, giving the man a baleful look. "You can help him all right, Nick. All the way to jail. He's the guy who shot Mack. Meet Lenny Farleigh."

Chapter 26

FOUR HOURS LATER she still sat in the police station, waiting for Mack. He'd been talking to the captain for the last little while. The other guy, the shooter, had been brought down to the station, along with her, but he'd been screaming about being attacked and wanting to press charges. Mack, she figured, was probably defending her to the captain. She wasn't too sure where she stood at this point in time, except that she stood by the fact that Lenny was Mack's shooter and that she had every right to hit him one or five times. He'd attacked her friend, and that was the end of it.

When Mack finally stepped out into the waiting area, he looked at her and frowned. She frowned right back, stiffened up, and crossed her arms over her chest.

Nick, at her side, reached over and patted her knee. "You'll be fine."

"Yeah, you're just saying that's because you're my lawyer."

At that, he burst out laughing.

"Besides, you're being paid to say that."

"Oh, you're paying me now?" he asked, with interest.

She glared at him and then, in a low voice, asked, "Am I really in trouble?"

"You did attack the man."

"Yes, I did. But I also knew he shot Mack and potentially me."

"What do you mean, he shot you?"

"What if he missed or what if he was trying to hit me with that first shot? Besides, he fired a second shot in my direction. Until we get to the bottom of all this mess, we don't have any idea what his plan was."

Nick pondered that for a moment. "And that could be part of your defense but not a big one though."

"Sure. And what was I supposed to do? Let him get away?"

"You could have called the police."

She looked at him, and her jaw dropped. "When? After he shot Mack and drove away from Rosemoor? Or right then at Mack's own house? I had already texted Mack the photos of the car and the license plate. That man *shot* Mack," she protested.

Nick nodded. "I get that you *think* he shot Mack."

She glared at him, her gaze narrowing.

"Are you really that sure?"

"I'm really that sure," she snapped. "And now we finally have a chance to figure out why this guy is after Mack."

"We have to prove it was him first."

"Then let me go talk to him," she muttered. "I'll prove it."

"It's not that simple," Nick warned.

"Why not?" she asked.

Mack now stood in front of her. "Because," he said, with exaggerated patience, "you attacked him."

She glared at him. "And what about the fact that he's the shooter everybody's hunting for?"

"Yes, that counts. Believe me. It counts. But it'll count more if we can *prove* he was the shooter."

She continued to glare at Mack. "And yet I can't help in the interrogation?"

"Nope, I promised the captain that you would not get involved."

She reached up with both hands and scrubbed her face. "That's not fair," she muttered. "I bring in the right guy, and now somehow we have to prove it's the right guy, just so I'm not in trouble."

At that, the captain stepped out, looked at her, and sighed. "You can't attack people."

She glared at him too. "So it's okay for Lenny to shoot Mack?"

The captain stared at her and asked, "Are you really that sure?"

"I am *really* that sure. Even more so are Mugs and Thaddeus and Goliath. They're the ones who led me to his car."

"But there was no car when we got there."

"Sure. He probably got somebody else to drive it away."

"You have any proof the car was there?" the captain asked.

She stopped, glowered at him, pulled out her phone, flicked up the photos, and then nodded. "Yes." And she handed her phone to him.

At that, he looked at her, snatched the phone from her hand, and nodded. "It's a silver Camry with the dent and those two letters in the license plate," the captain agreed. "That changes things, but it still doesn't mean he was the one driving it."

"No, I was supposed to apparently wait until he got in the car and drove away," she said, with an eye roll. The chief gave her an exaggerated look. She raised both hands in frustration. "He *shot* Mack," she reiterated.

"And because of that, we'll hold him, but we must have a reason to hold him past forty-eight hours."

She frowned. "So why I can't help sort this out?"

"You're already in a mess," said the captain in a stern voice. "You need to let the police handle this."

She bit her bottom lip and looked over at Mack. "And you should be home resting. You should never have picked me up in the first place with your injured arm."

He rolled his eyes at that. "You were beating him up."

"And he was coming to kill you."

"He was trying to get away," Mack snapped.

"Sure he was," she said, glaring at him, "*after* I'd already caught him."

At that, knowing that they wouldn't get anywhere, Mack looked over at the captain. "I promise I'll keep her at home."

"Good." The captain sighed, turned to face her, and asked, "How did you find this guy?"

"He was casing Mack's place. I took Mugs out to Mack's backyard, so he could go to the bathroom. When he was done, I went into the alley and put the doggie bag into the garbage can, and then Mugs and Goliath both took off, only to stop at this car. I realized instantly whose car it was, and, when I headed up the alleyway to get back to Mack, this guy was racing toward his car. And I had like a split second to make a decision, so I plowed him one. And then he started calling me crazy and all kinds of other names, so I plowed into him again. That's when he really started getting angry, and then he started to fight back."

"He told me that he was trying to get away from you."

She frowned at that. "You know what? I think he said something about he just wanted to get away. But then, of course, anybody would say that."

"You were attacking him," Mack reminded her, his lips twitching.

She glared at him. "Absolutely I was," she said, her arms across her chest again. "Remember that part about him shooting you?" At that, she looked up to see the shooter being moved from one room to another.

He took one look at her and screamed, "You. You're the crazy woman who jumped me."

She hopped to her feet. Mack immediately reached out and grabbed her and winced. She glared at Mack. "See? I told you that you shouldn't be using your bad arm." She looked back at the shooter. "And you are the crazy idiot who shot Chuck and Mack."

At that, the color drained from Lenny's face.

"What?" He looked back at the others. "No, no, no, no, no. No way do you know anything about that."

Every cop in the room stiffened.

"They might not know about it, but I do. And you, *sir*, are not getting away with this. You should never have touched Mack."

He glared at her. "You don't understand. This is bigger than you."

"It sure is," she snapped, still standing with Mack, his arm around her, trying to hold her back. "And, if you don't start talking, you'll be lucky if you have anybody else to talk to ever again," she cried out. "Chuck is already in the hospital and doesn't look like he'll make it. Thankfully Mack survived, but, if you think coming back around for a second try will get you anywhere, you're wrong."

"And what does it matter to you, you stupid woman?" he roared. "You and that crazy loony-tune zoo of yours, you're all nuts."

"Sure, but we're in good company, so who cares?"

He stared at her and then shook his head. "See what I mean? She doesn't make any sense. You can't even listen to her."

"Oh, they listen to me just fine," she said in a very low tone. "You waited for Mack that evening outside Rosemoor, and you shot him."

"Yeah? And why would I want to do that?"

"I haven't got all the answers yet, but I got a lot of them."

He snorted. "You don't have any answers. You're just crazy."

"It depends whether Chuck wakes up enough to talk to us or not, and, of course, I scared Dante with my telephone call, so he is ready to run off at the mouth."

Lenny stared at her in shock. "No, Dante wouldn't do that. We were all in this together."

"Really?" she murmured in a bored tone of voice. "You see? You guys always put such faith in the wrong people."

"No, Dante won't do that. He's got too much to lose."

"Yeah, I know about the original scheme. Rodney was taking bribes back then, some fifteen years ago, and he's part of the criminal case that came up against his old grandpa Vaughn."

"Old Grandpa Vaughn was guilty," Lenny snapped. "So were a lot of people back then. It was like a big dragnet. If you didn't fight what they were doing, then you were in collusion. So most of us did time for that nightmare."

"I agree with you," Doreen stated, "but his son Terrance Bowman, who skipped out on jail time because he died before it could happen, was in the mix as well. But also guilty is that woman everybody thought was too young to be a criminal and who eventually married the grandson, Rodney. Your sister, Celia."

Lenny stared at her. "How can you know all that?"

"Because I talk to people." She shrugged. "And I put pieces together." She turned toward the captain. "Did you find two phones on Lenny?"

The captain frowned at her. "Yes."

"I suspect one is his own, but the other one will be Chuck's. Lenny shot Chuck and then stole his phone."

"Nope, nope, nope." Lenny shook his head. "I'm not listening. What's that got to do with me?"

"Your latest scheme. Blackmail."

At that, the color immediately drained from his face. He looked at the captain. "You don't understand," he cried out. "If Rodney finds out I'm one of those blackmailing him, he'll kill me."

"Really?" the captain asked. "So you tried to kill a cop, and now you're worried about these criminals killing you? What do you think we'll all have to say about it?"

Lenny stared at her and back at the captain. "Look. I'll tell you everything, but you have to protect me."

"And why is that?" the captain asked in a bored tone of voice that easily matched Mack's at times.

"Because they'll come after me, and they'll kill me and Nettie. She's a good woman. The best part of this messed up family. Of course she's adopted, not blood, so maybe that explains it."

"Yeah? Why don't you tell us who it is we're dealing with," the captain explained. "Because, if we don't get all the information, no way we can help you."

The shooter stared at Doreen, with loathing. "And you keep her away from me. She's crazy."

The captain winced at that. "I can do my best on that point, but not even Mack can keep her completely corralled."

She snorted at that. "Especially not when you shot Mack. Why Mack? Why after all this time?" Then something random hit her. "I got it!" she cried out. "You did time with Pauly, right?"

His jaw dropped. "How do you know that name? No one calls Dante that."

"Nettie does." She nodded, seeing his face blanch. "Is she part of this too?"

"No," he cried out. "My niece has nothing to do with this. Honest." Lenny paused, then continued. "Look we were all guilty to a certain extent back then, except Chuck—who got in trouble later when he got caught up in something else. But when Dante got out, he was broke. He hooked up with Chuck, only neither had money or a job. So the two of them dreamt up a blackmail scheme, based on insider info they got in prison about people avoiding jail, staying under the radar. And I wanted in on the action."

At that Mack stiffened beside her.

She sympathized with him. It was hard to hear such things about two old friends. "Of course they did. It's easy money and hard to change your ways when you're fresh out of jail and when it's a struggle to find gainful employment."

"Exactly." Lenny groaned. "But they blackmailed the wrong people."

She nodded slowly. "They blackmailed Rodney and Celia. Over the stepson." Doreen turned to Mack. "This is the connection between fifteen years ago and now. Simply that the Bowmans were involved in the prior construction con, as the perpetrators, and now the Bowmans are involved in this current blackmail scheme, as the victims."

Lenny stared at her. "Jesus, how do you know all this?"

She gave him a hard smile. "Keep talking."

"Rodney paid the ransom a couple times, then realized it would never end."

"And why Mack?"

He winced. "Because Chuck said that he would sic Mack on Rodney and that Mack always listened to Chuck and that Mack was responsible for me and my partner Vaughn going down the last time. And Rodney decided, I guess, that Chuck and Mack should be taken out of it."

"What do you mean, *you guess?*" Doreen's eyebrows shot up. "You're the one who shot both of them. But why come back a second time? Why show up at Mack's house? Or better question yet, why did you shoot him in the first place?"

Lenny just stared at her and clenched his jaw.

She nodded. "Because Rodney had something on you too. He's the one who insisted you finish the job."

He nodded slowly. "Yeah, he does have something on me, and he blackmailed me into it. But, when I failed, he wouldn't let up, saying I had to finish the job or else." He nodded. "I did shoot them, but I didn't mean to kill Chuck. Or Mack." Lenny shot a glance Mack's way.

"That's good because you failed at both. Hate to see you get a second chance."

At that, he stared at her, bewildered. "Hey, I was into

construction schemes, later blackmail, not murder. I was supposed to kill both of them. I freaked out when I saw all the blood coming from Chuck. So I really didn't want to do it again. Yet Rodney won't take no from anybody. He's threatened to kill me and Nettie. So I … I tried. I trashed talked Mack to give me some self-confidence. But you were there with Mack. And those animals. I got nervous and missed."

Doreen shook her head. "So you shot your own criminal buddy Chuck down in Vancouver. You must have known that bar was a routine hangout of his, being so close to where you both lived and all. Then the very next day you shot Mack, and I want to know how you knew he was going to be at Rosemoor that evening?"

Lenny snorted. "Kelowna is a small place. Gossip flows. If you go anywhere, I heard talk about the *celebration of Doreen* scheduled for that night. I'd gone into Rosemoor to ask more about it, but I didn't even need to ask anyone, as they had posters up, reminding all the residents that the two of you and the dratted zoo would be there that particular night. Luckily I've been gone for so long that nobody recognized me. All I had to do was wait for Mack that night."

"And so you were involved with Chuck and Dante blackmailing Rodney."

Lenny hung his head. "Yeah."

Doreen continued. "Then somehow Rodney found out that Chuck and you were his blackmailers."

Lenny sighed. "Don't know how he found out, but yeah."

Doreen laughed. "You were blackmailing your sister's husband, which is odd enough. Then I figured out that

Celia's son, Rodney's stepson, is actually his grandfather's child. That makes the teenager Vaughn's son, who has more rights to the family inheritance than Rodney does, right?"

Lenny swallowed hard and nodded. "Yeah, but I don't have a clue how you figured it out."

"Human nature," she said. "And what did Rodney have on you that you were prepared to kill a cop to keep hidden?"

Lenny's face scrunched up, and it looked like he would cry.

"No, you don't get to back out on this point," she snapped. "Not when you shot my friend to keep it hidden."

He groaned. "I just wanted to put it all behind me. I did my time. Stupid as I was, I didn't get caught for all my crimes back then, and Rodney said he knew how to bring all those charges back up against me, and this time I'd go away for good."

"And you didn't consider that shooting a cop would send you away forever regardless?" Now he really looked like he would cry.

"I have information on Rodney and Celia. Not to mention quite a few other people. Honest. I'm happy to share it all." He looked at Mack and the captain pleadingly, but Doreen wasn't prepared to let him off the hook yet.

"What about Dante? Did he have anything to do with Mack getting shot?"

Lenny slowly shook his head. "No, I shot Mack. Rodney was behind that."

"And Celia?" Doreen was adamant that no one forgot her role in all this.

Lenny winced. "Yeah, she's worse than Rodney. But you'd never know it. Look. She may be my sister, and we were all friends back then, but things change. Most of us did a little time over that construction mess and stayed in touch. Most of us were in the slammer together one time or another. Not Celia though. She's the kind butter won't melt in her mouth, but she'd stab you in the back if it would improve her world."

"I'm sure she would," Doreen agreed. "And I'm pretty sure she also did her best to send her father-in-law to jail too—likely for getting her pregnant and refusing to marry her."

"I wouldn't be at all surprised. She may be my sister, but she's still scary. You have to protect me," he whispered hoarsely, looking over at the captain. "I'll tell you what you want to know, but you have to keep me and Nettie alive."

At that, the captain studied him, looked over at Doreen and sighed.

"You can pick up Rodney at any time. He's local." She beamed at him. "Now go pick up Dante. I understand he may live in Vancouver, in the same general neighborhood that Chuck lives in. However, you'll probably find he's in town too."

"And why is that?" Mack asked, his arm still around her, pulling her closer.

She turned, wrapped her arms around Mack. "Because I'm pretty sure, at this point in time, he thinks he's the next one to be shot, and he's here to stave it off. With you shot, and Chuck down, Rodney knows Dante's the only other blackmailer still alive, who was involved in the construction mess from so long ago. Or does Dante prefer to be called Pauly?"

He swallowed and nodded. "I don't know how you know that either," he cried out.

"Nettie said something that made me wonder. Besides,

Dante is the only blackmailer left. So he leads the top of the hit list from Rodney's perspective. Somehow Rodney found out that Dante and Chuck and Lenny were his blackmailers. So, of course, Rodney is hunting Lenny and now Dante, what with Chuck possibly dying in the hospital." She looked at the captain. "You better get out there fast to pick up Dante *and* Rodney."

And, with that, the captain issued orders. And when he was done, he turned, looked at the three of them—Nick, Mack, and Doreen—and said, "Take her home. And, Mack, stay out of trouble."

Mack looked at him in surprise. "*Me* stay out of trouble?"

"Anytime you're with Doreen, you get into trouble too." The captain shook his head. "The two of you make a great pair, so why don't you finally make it official?"

And, with that, the captain turned and walked away.

Chapter 27

MACK, NICK, AND Doreen and her animals ended up going back to Doreen's house. And in two separate vehicles. She drove home and got there first. She turned off the alarm system, headed inside, and immediately put on coffee. She was unsettled and stressed. She opened the rear kitchen door and let the animals out before her, as she stood on the deck and rubbed her temples. "Good Lord, Doreen," she muttered, "this one is all kinds of bad."

For the first time ever, she'd actually gone on the attack, and that was something so foreign to her nature that she didn't even know what to think about it. She was sure any shrink would have a heyday with her. But, as far as she was concerned, it really had to do with the fact that somebody had hurt a friend of hers. Somebody had hurt Mack. She couldn't imagine what it would be like if it were Nan. And, of course, Nan had been hurt recently, but not to the extent of getting shot by a gun. Then she heard footsteps at her front door, the brothers Moreau had finally arrived.

She walked over, opened the door, and asked, "What took you so long?" Then she smelled the pizza. She sniffed the air and cried out, "Oh my God, food."

Mack stepped inside, reached out, and not even giving her a chance to argue, pulled her in for a hug. And he just held her close.

Behind him, she heard Nick saying, "Coming through, coming through." And he lifted the pizza boxes over their heads and carried on to the kitchen.

With that, now realizing that she really could just relax, she cuddled into Mack's arms. When she pulled her head back, she looked up at him. "What's that hug for?"

"Because you needed one." He tilted her chin, leaned down, and kissed her gently. "*That*," he whispered, "is for caring."

"Oh," she said in a small voice. "You're not angry at me anymore?"

His lips quirked. "You do test my patience, but the one thing that I do know and always have known," he added, "is you come from heart. Even the captain knows that."

She sighed. "They'll bug you mercilessly about me and you, won't they?"

"Yep, they sure will."

She grinned. "Good," she announced. "That'll keep you in line."

He sighed, reached out, tapped her on the nose. "But we're still not out of danger, until we can pick up Rodney and Celia. However, the little bird Dante aka Pauly, is sitting in a jail cell, singing quite freely, and he has a lot to sing about."

"Good." She beamed at him. "And you brought food, so that's even better."

He burst out laughing. "My brother's hungry."

She looked toward the kitchen, then at Mack. "But Nick shares, right?"

Mack's grin widened, and he looped his good arm around her and nudged her forward. "He absolutely does. Come on. Let's go eat."

And they walked toward the kitchen and to the open back door and found Nick sitting outside, surrounded by open boxes of pizza.

He looked up when they came. "And here I thought I would get it all for myself."

"Not in this lifetime," she declared immediately, as she sat down beside him and sniffed the pizzas. "Mack's corrupted me to pizza. I had so little of anything like this in my life, before him, but now ..." She eyed the slices avariciously.

"You're certainly getting your share of it now," Mack stated peaceably, as he reached across and snagged the biggest piece from one box.

She watched as Nick reached for the next biggest piece, and then Doreen realized that it really was fair, as they were bigger than she was, and they had bought the pizzas. So she was a good girl and reached across and picked up the third-biggest piece.

"It was hard to do that, wasn't it?" Mack teased her.

She rolled her eyes. "I'm trying to remember my manners. Since I met you, it's all gone out the window."

He stopped and stared at her. "Since you met me?"

"Yeah." She nodded. "I used to be perfect."

He grinned. "If that was perfect, I prefer this version."

"This one's kind of unfettered," she muttered around her first bite. "Cut loose. She found freedom, and, so far, she hasn't really figured out how to control certain aspects of her world."

"And that's fine," Mack told her gently. "Remember? It'll take time."

"You have more patience than I do. I should have figured it out by now."

He smiled and looked over at his brother and nodded toward her. "I was telling you about that."

"I know." Nick studied her face. "I just never met such a free spirit before. Not like this."

"And you probably won't ever again, unless you meet Nan," Doreen muttered. "Honestly, I probably wouldn't be like this, except for all the years with my ex."

"I can understand that." Then Nick added, "Your ex also sent back a second offer."

She stopped, her mouth open, pizza midair. "Seriously?"

He nodded. "Wow, you actually got him to negotiate."

"More or less. Of course we have a long way to go before we come to a meeting of minds on any of this," he noted, "but he's talking."

"Still, that's progress." Doreen was amazed. "You must be good."

"Of course I'm good." Nick stared at her in surprise. "Isn't that why you hired me?"

"Considering you came for free." She gave him a cheeky grin. She let her voice trail off, as she beamed at him.

He just shook his head at her, looked over at Mack, and said, "She just never quits with the insults, does she?"

"No, it's all part of that unfettered freedom right now," Mack explained. "Most of the time she's completely harmless."

"Yeah, tell that to the guy she caught in the alleyway," Nick muttered.

She looked at Nick worriedly. "Lenny will be okay, won't he?"

"Yep."

At that, Mack reached across, picked up her hand, and looked at her scraped-up knuckles. "We'll have to teach you how to punch the right way. You hit like a girl."

She glared at him. "Maybe like a girl, but I still got my guy."

He laughed. "Yeah, you sure did." He squeezed her hand affectionately. "Now we just must ensure that getting your guy doesn't mean getting caught by the cops. And ending up with charges."

"I know." She stared down at the pizza in her hand. "I guess I kind of skated on that one."

"You absolutely did. But, in your view, you were justified, and I'm sure a jury would have let you off on that too. I just don't know how much more tolerance the captain has."

"He's been good to me so far, and I'm not *trying* to be difficult. I *am* trying to help."

"I know, but your version of help is not exactly the version he wants."

She didn't know what to say. Finally she said, "It's not over though, is it?"

"No, not yet. They have to pick up everybody who's not already in custody. I haven't had an update yet."

"Right."

Almost immediately Mack got a text. He looked down and smiled. "Celia's been picked up. Rodney's at large. So that's two out of three.'

"Good," Doreen replied. "You should probably get ready though, Mack."

"For what?" Nick looked at her in surprise.

She sighed. "Rodney will be coming here."

"Who?" Nick asked, startled.

"Rodney."

Both men stared at her in shock.

"Why?" Nick asked.

"Because he'll blame either me or Mack. It won't take him long to figure out where we are."

Nick looked over at her. "Isn't he the one who almost took your door off?"

"Yeah, I know it's kind of worrisome—especially when we don't really know when he'll attack."

"You also don't know *that* he will attack." Mack pointed a finger at her. "Don't let your imagination run away with you."

"What? Do you think we need any more clues?" she asked, with a cheeky grin.

And just then a voice behind her snapped, "What you need is a bullet. You're too smart for your own good."

She looked at Mack to see him staring at somebody behind her. "So, Mack, how'd I do? Did I call it or what?"

"You called it." Mack slowly put down his pizza. "At least most of it."

And that made her realize that somebody else was involved.

"Do I get to turn around and see who is there?" Slowly she twisted in her chair, pizza still in her hand, as she stared at two men. She studied them for a moment. "Did you come to shoot me?"

"That's what you deserve," Rodney snapped, pointing a larger handgun than she was used to.

"Hello, Rodney. I can't say I'm happy to see you again." She studied the other man. "You're family too, so you're both connected to this mess."

"Sure am." The other guy gave her a sour look.

"And, if you hadn't come today, chances are you would

have got off scot-free because we didn't know about you."

"You would have got around to me eventually."

At that, Mack looked at the second man in shock. Then, as if pulling a name from the back of his brain, he asked, "Wilson?"

He glared at him. "Yeah. See? Like I said, you would have got around to me eventually." He stared down at Doreen. "And you're right. We're family. Cousins."

Mack stared at him. "You always hated me anyway."

"Sure did. You were the football hero. You were the jock. The girls loved you."

Mack shook his head. "No, not quite. Just one girl back then." He looked over at Doreen. He shrugged. "We were high school sweethearts, but this guy really wanted her too."

"Hey, it just sowed the seeds of discontent way back when," Wilson said. "When I heard Rodney was coming here, gunning for your lady, I had to come take a look."

"What makes you think I'm his lady?" she asked. "Besides, we picked up your shooter, Lenny. He and Dante are talking to the cops."

"They are idiots. Nobody listens to them."

"Oh, I think the cops are listening right now, cutting a deal."

"That's fine," Rodney replied. "We'll pop them as soon as they get loose."

"Why did you wait so long for this supposed revenge?" Mack asked.

"It wouldn't even have come to this, except for those stupid idiots turning to blackmail. Dante, Lenny, and Chuck—all idiots. That's what happens when stupid multiplies. They come out of jail. They don't know how to make an honest living, so they turn back to what they do know. They figure out who's got the money, and that's where they go. Just like homing pigeons." Rodney stared at her. "You think you're pretty smart, don't you?"

"No. Determined? Yes. A little bit tenacious? Yes. Kind of …" She winced. "Focused and maybe a little OCD? Yes, but I don't think I come up very high on any intelligence list."

Mack frowned at her; so did Nick.

But she ignored them, staring over at the other two men. "On the other hand, when it comes to loyalty, I can't be beat."

"Loyalty is worth a lot," Rodney agreed. "Too bad you won't ever get a chance to be loyal to another person."

"Oh, I don't know. I get that you think you're in a free-for-all here, that you'll just shoot all three of us, that nobody will ever know, and then it's done. Except your wife's been picked up, Rodney. And the cops are all over town looking for you."

At that, Rodney stared at her. "My wife?"

"Yeah, you haven't checked in on Celia in a while, have you? She was picked up about an hour ago."

His eyes widened in horror. "No way, no way. You don't understand. If that happens, there will be consequences."

"Oh, I do understand." She smiled. "And even more so now that she has been picked up. I'm not lying about that."

Rodney immediately cocked his gun, as if ready to fire.

"You might want to look down before you do that," Doreen suggested.

"Why?" He looked down immediately and then back up at her.

She nodded. "You don't understand. When I said I understand loyalty, it wasn't just how loyal I am but also about the others who love me and who are loyal to me."

He looked down again, and there was Mugs, sitting on his butt, staring up at him, a growl deep in his throat.

"This thing? I could kick him from here into tomorrow." He laughed.

"You might, but you will lose that foot if you do."

At that, he burst out laughing. He pulled his right leg back, as if to kick Mugs.

Wilson started to laugh too. "Good God, is she for real?"

"We'll see," Rodney muttered. And his foot came forward at a speed that made her stare at him, but Mugs was no longer there. Matter of fact Mugs had jumped at the one target he'd been eyeing right in front of him. Mugs latched onto Rodney's groin, and Rodney went down, screaming in agony, the gun going off harmlessly.

Mack was already in motion, as Wilson stared at Rodney in shock, trying to figure out what had just happened. But by the time Wilson lifted his gun, it was already too late. Mack and Nick grabbed him, and Doreen had already picked up Rodney's gun that had skittered across the deck.

Wilson fought for control of his gun, screaming, "I'll shoot her and end this."

Doreen turned the gun in his direction. "You really think I'll let you shoot anybody else?"

Mack turned, looked at her, and froze. "Doreen, put that down."

She immediately shook her head. "You get that gun away from him first," she snapped. "He'll shoot Mugs."

At that, the Moreau brothers realized—with Rodney bawling like a baby on the deck, hunched up in a fetal position—that Mugs had turned his attention to the second man.

Wilson snapped. "I'll shoot the stupid dog."

Before he had a chance to say anything more, Goliath jumped up, claws extended, and landed on Wilson's back. Goliath dug in his claws, as gravity dragged the weight of his body downward, ripping up Wilson's back. Wilson screamed, falling to his knees.

Mack dropped him all the way down to the ground and put a foot on his back. "Now stay there." He leaned over and, with his good arm, pulled the gun away from Wilson. He looked over at Doreen. "Call the animals back."

She immediately made a sharp whistle, and Goliath hopped up casually, adding further insult as he walked over the guy's head, landing each clawed paw on top of Wilson's scalp, before sauntering toward her. Mugs raced toward her, barking happily, his tail helicoptering with joy.

Mack looked around. "*Uh-oh*, where is Thaddeus?"

At the mention of his name, Thaddeus went for a dive bomb off her shoulder, skittering down toward the two men lying beside each other on the deck. In a move Doreen had never seen him do before, Thaddeus splatted a double shot of poop on each man's forehead, before landing a few feet away in the grass.

She looked at Thaddeus, turned to Nick and Mack. "Oh my." And then she burst out laughing.

Mack stared at the animals. "I would not have believed it …"

"I was here," Nick admitted. "I saw it firsthand, and *I* don't believe it."

Mack looked at Doreen. "You really are mad." She immediately dropped the laughter and glared at him. He held up his hands. "But it's a good mad. You and the animals are one heck of a team."

"And the lesson here," she replied triumphantly, "is don't hurt anybody I care about, and nobody is allowed to hurt me either."

Epilogue

Early September

IT SEEMED LIKE the days had whipped past since that last chaotic scenario at Doreen's house. Today she sat by the water at her wonderful bench addition, a cup of coffee in her hand, Nick on one side and Mack on the other. She turned toward Mack. "How's physio going?"

"Better. Apparently, I escaped a pretty ugly shoulder injury."

"Good." She hesitated and then asked, "And how about the two guys who showed up here?"

"Rodney has stitches in a region no man should ever have stitches," Mack stated, shuddering, "but should make a full recovery, and then goes directly to jail."

"And the other man, Wilson?"

"He'll have long welts for quite a few more days on his back and head, but he's already in jail," Mack told her. "What I want to know is, how did you train Thaddeus to drop bird poop on your attackers like that?"

She winced. "I didn't train Thaddeus. He did that all on his own."

Mack just shook his head, as he considered the bird even

now wandering in front of them on the pathway, standing on rocks, hopping off rocks. "Thaddeus looks totally harmless now."

Doreen laughed.

Meanwhile, Goliath and Mugs lay in the sun, basking, just being the heroes they were.

"You know what? I've seen these animals respond in more ways with you than I ever thought possible," Mack stated. "Yet I had no idea they could do what they did this last time."

"Neither did I," she replied. "And I mean it. It's all about loyalty. And, for whatever reason, I've been blessed to have their love *and* their loyalty. And I try hard to never do anything to damage that."

At that, Nick patted her on the shoulder and stated, "Not just *their* love. A lot of people in town love you too."

She gave him a sad smile. "But apparently a lot more people in town also don't love me," she admitted, "so it's been a mixed blessing."

Nick smiled. "Eventually you will find a lot of people on your side versus the other side."

"I suppose," she agreed. "It just takes time."

The two brothers nodded.

"And I need to get the captain back on my side," she added. "I'm not exactly sure how to do that though."

"It's not that he's *not* on your side," Mack argued cautiously. "He just needs you to stay out of our cases when it comes to the legal stuff, so that he can get a case nailed down and so that enough criminals don't walk because of problems with the collection of evidence." He sent her a knowing look.

"Right," she said, "all that legal stuff."

"I get that the legal stuff isn't a big deal for you," Mack cautioned her, "but we don't want to do all this work and have these guys go free."

She nodded. "I could be very good for a few days," she suggested. "Maybe the captain will forgive me then."

"Nothing to forgive, just keep a low profile," Mack stated.

"Right. I might be able to do that." Doreen studied Mack for a moment. "You're off for a few more days. How about we try paddleboarding again? If your physio allows it …" She turned toward Nick. "I don't know where we'd get a board for you, but, if you want to come with us, that would be awesome."

"That sounds great." Nick nodded, raising his coffee cup in agreement.

And, just when the guys were getting up to leave, a vehicle drove up, and she said, "*Uh-oh.*"

"What's *uh-oh?*" Mack asked.

"That's the captain's vehicle."

"Oh." Mack walked over to talk to him.

Doreen stepped through the house and out on the front porch and asked the captain, "Problems?"

"Not so many problems," the captain began, "but I wondered if I could speak with you."

She looked surprised but replied, "Absolutely."

"*Uhm,*" the captain added, "and possibly alone, if I could."

She looked over at Mack, who shrugged and said, "We were just leaving." At that, Mack and Nick got into their vehicle. Mack made a sign for her to call him later.

She smiled and nodded and led the captain into her house. "Do you want a coffee?"

He hesitated and then nodded. "If you wouldn't mind. I kind of …" He hesitated again.

"Am I in trouble?" she asked immediately.

He looked at her in surprise and then smiled. "No, you're not. Yet, because of the trouble you *do* get into, I have a favor to ask."

She frowned. "Okay, sure. What can I do for you?"

"It's a cold case."

She beamed. "I would love to work on another cold case."

"It involves my cousin. He was killed several years ago. In fact, he was shot in the garden."

"In the garden?" she asked, liking the idea already, but careful to keep the smile off her face.

"Yeah, in the sunflowers," he added.

"Ooh," she replied, "the *Silenced in the Sunflowers* case."

He slowly nodded. "I guess, if that's how you want to look at it."

She nodded. "That's how I want to look at it. I need details, more details." Doreen clasped her hands together to keep from rubbing them with glee, as she shot him a look. "And you'll forgive me for attacking Lenny if I solve this cold case?"

He laughed. "Nothing to forgive. It's because of your unique viewpoint and your way of coming at things that I'm here right now. If you can help me with this case," the captain stated, "believe me. I'll be in your debt."

"*Silenced in the Sunflowers*, here we come," she cried out.

At that, Mugs barked, Goliath howled, and Thaddeus repeated her words with joy.

This concludes Book 18 of Lovely Lethal Gardens:
Revenge in the Roses.

Read about Silenced in the Sunflowers: Lovely Lethal
Gardens, Book 19

Lovely Lethal Gardens: Silenced in the Sunflowers (Book #19)

A new cozy mystery series from *USA Today* best-selling author Dale Mayer. Follow gardener and amateur sleuth Doreen Montgomery—and her amusing and mostly lovable cat, dog, and parrot—as they catch murderers and solve crimes in lovely Kelowna, British Columbia.

Riches to rags. … Hearts start to heal. … Friendships start to grow, … just not for everyone!

Doreen knows her relationship with the police captain has always been on thin ground. She has helped them solve a lot of cases, but she's quadrupled their work and constantly gets in their way. So no one is more surprised than Doreen when the captain stops by and asks for a personal favor, concerning a cold case from his own childhood.

Slowly recovering from his injury, Corporal Mack Moreau learns that the captain has stopped by Doreen's house, asking for a moment of her time. Curious, Mack's even more stunned to hear the details about his captain's visit. Mack wants to help, but investigating a case from forty years ago doesn't leave much behind to go on.

Doreen knows that failing to solve a case has to happen *sometime*. But she'd do a lot to not have that happen here, not when the captain had personally asked for her help. So, with her critters in tow, Doreen is off and running, ... leaving Mack watching—and worrying—in her wake.

Find Book 19 here!

To find out more visit Dale Mayer's website.

https://smarturl.it/DMSilencedUniversal

Get Your Free Book Now!

Have you met Charmin Marvin?

If you're ready for a new world to explore, and love ill-mannered cats, I have a series that might be your next binge read. It's called Broken Protocols, and it's a series that takes you through time-travel, mysteries, romance… and a talking cat named Charmin Marvin.

Go here and tell me where to send it!
http://smarturl.it/ArsenicBofB

Author's Note

Thank you for reading Revenge in the Roses: Lovely Lethal Gardens, Book 18! If you enjoyed the book, please take a moment and leave a short review.

Dear reader,

I love to hear from readers, and you can contact me at my website: www.dalemayer.com or at my Facebook author page. To be informed of new releases and special offers, sign up for my newsletter or follow me on BookBub. And if you are interested in joining Dale Mayer's Reader Group, here is the Facebook sign up page.
https://smarturl.it/DaleMayerFBGroup

Cheers,
Dale Mayer

About the Author

Dale Mayer is a *USA Today* best-selling author, best known for her SEALs military romances, her Psychic Visions series, and her Lovely Lethal Garden cozy series. Her contemporary romances are raw and full of passion and emotion (Broken But … Mending, Hathaway House series). Her thrillers will keep you guessing (Kate Morgan, By Death series), and her romantic comedies will keep you giggling (*It's a Dog's Life*, a stand-alone novella; and the Broken Protocols series, starring Charming Marvin, the cat).

Dale honors the stories that come to her—and some of them are crazy, break all the rules and cross multiple genres!

To go with her fiction, she also writes nonfiction in many different fields, with books available on résumé writing, companion gardening, and the US mortgage system. All her books are available in print and ebook format.

Connect with Dale Mayer Online

Dale's Website – www.dalemayer.com
Twitter – @DaleMayer
Facebook Page – geni.us/DaleMayerFBFanPage
Facebook Group – geni.us/DaleMayerFBGroup
BookBub – geni.us/DaleMayerBookbub
Instagram – geni.us/DaleMayerInstagram
Goodreads – geni.us/DaleMayerGoodreads
Newsletter – geni.us/DaleNews

Also by Dale Mayer

Published Adult Books:

Shadow Recon
Magnus, Book 1

Bullard's Battle
Ryland's Reach, Book 1
Cain's Cross, Book 2
Eton's Escape, Book 3
Garret's Gambit, Book 4
Kano's Keep, Book 5
Fallon's Flaw, Book 6
Quinn's Quest, Book 7
Bullard's Beauty, Book 8
Bullard's Best, Book 9
Bullard's Battle, Books 1–2
Bullard's Battle, Books 3–4
Bullard's Battle, Books 5–6
Bullard's Battle, Books 7–8

Terkel's Team
Damon's Deal, Book 1
Wade's War, Book 2
Gage's Goal, Book 3
Calum's Contact, Book 4
Rick's Road, Book 5

Psychic Vision Series

Itsy-Bitsy Spider
Unmasked
Deep Beneath
From the Ashes
Stroke of Death
Ice Maiden
Snap, Crackle...
What If...
Talking Bones
String of Tears
Psychic Visions Books 1–3
Psychic Visions Books 4–6
Psychic Visions Books 7–9

By Death Series
Touched by Death
Haunted by Death
Chilled by Death
By Death Books 1–3

Broken Protocols – Romantic Comedy Series
Cat's Meow
Cat's Pajamas
Cat's Cradle
Cat's Claus
Broken Protocols 1-4

Broken and... Mending
Skin
Scars
Scales (of Justice)
Broken but... Mending 1-3

Glory

Genesis
Tori
Celeste
Glory Trilogy

Biker Blues

Morgan: Biker Blues, Volume 1
Cash: Biker Blues, Volume 2

SEALs of Honor

Mason: SEALs of Honor, Book 1
Hawk: SEALs of Honor, Book 2
Dane: SEALs of Honor, Book 3
Swede: SEALs of Honor, Book 4
Shadow: SEALs of Honor, Book 5
Cooper: SEALs of Honor, Book 6
Markus: SEALs of Honor, Book 7
Evan: SEALs of Honor, Book 8
Mason's Wish: SEALs of Honor, Book 9
Chase: SEALs of Honor, Book 10
Brett: SEALs of Honor, Book 11
Devlin: SEALs of Honor, Book 12
Easton: SEALs of Honor, Book 13
Ryder: SEALs of Honor, Book 14
Macklin: SEALs of Honor, Book 15
Corey: SEALs of Honor, Book 16
Warrick: SEALs of Honor, Book 17
Tanner: SEALs of Honor, Book 18
Jackson: SEALs of Honor, Book 19
Kanen: SEALs of Honor, Book 20
Nelson: SEALs of Honor, Book 21

Taylor: SEALs of Honor, Book 22
Colton: SEALs of Honor, Book 23
Troy: SEALs of Honor, Book 24
Axel: SEALs of Honor, Book 25
Baylor: SEALs of Honor, Book 26
Hudson: SEALs of Honor, Book 27
Lachlan: SEALs of Honor, Book 28
Paxton: SEALs of Honor, Book 29
SEALs of Honor, Books 1–3
SEALs of Honor, Books 4–6
SEALs of Honor, Books 7–10
SEALs of Honor, Books 11–13
SEALs of Honor, Books 14–16
SEALs of Honor, Books 17–19
SEALs of Honor, Books 20–22
SEALs of Honor, Books 23–25

Heroes for Hire
Levi's Legend: Heroes for Hire, Book 1
Stone's Surrender: Heroes for Hire, Book 2
Merk's Mistake: Heroes for Hire, Book 3
Rhodes's Reward: Heroes for Hire, Book 4
Flynn's Firecracker: Heroes for Hire, Book 5
Logan's Light: Heroes for Hire, Book 6
Harrison's Heart: Heroes for Hire, Book 7
Saul's Sweetheart: Heroes for Hire, Book 8
Dakota's Delight: Heroes for Hire, Book 9
Tyson's Treasure: Heroes for Hire, Book 10
Jace's Jewel: Heroes for Hire, Book 11
Rory's Rose: Heroes for Hire, Book 12
Brandon's Bliss: Heroes for Hire, Book 13
Liam's Lily: Heroes for Hire, Book 14

SEALs of Steel

Dare to Love…
Dare to be Strong…
RomanceX3

Standalone Novellas
It's a Dog's Life
Riana's Revenge
Second Chances

Published Young Adult Books:

Family Blood Ties Series
Vampire in Denial
Vampire in Distress
Vampire in Design
Vampire in Deceit
Vampire in Defiance
Vampire in Conflict
Vampire in Chaos
Vampire in Crisis
Vampire in Control
Vampire in Charge
Family Blood Ties Set 1–3
Family Blood Ties Set 1–5
Family Blood Ties Set 4–6
Family Blood Ties Set 7–9
Sian's Solution, A Family Blood Ties Series Prequel
    Novelette

Design series
Dangerous Designs
Deadly Designs

Darkest Designs
Design Series Trilogy

Standalone
In Cassie's Corner
Gem Stone (a Gemma Stone Mystery)
Time Thieves

Published Non-Fiction Books:

Career Essentials
Career Essentials: The Résumé
Career Essentials: The Cover Letter
Career Essentials: The Interview
Career Essentials: 3 in 1

Made in United States
North Haven, CT
04 August 2022